Eleven Letters

Sally Measom

Eleven Letters

Copyright © Sally Measom 2025

The moral right of Sally Measom to be identified as the author of this work has been asserted in accordance with the Copyright, Designs and Patents Act 1988.

All rights reserved. No part of this book may be reproduced or used in any manner whatsoever, including information storage and retrieval systems, or transmitted in any form or by any means, electronic, mechanical, photocopying, recording or otherwise, without the express written permission of the copyright owner, except in the case of brief quotations embodied in critical reviews and certain other non-commercial use permitted by copyright law. For permission requests, contact the author at the address below.

References to historical events, real people, or real places are used fictitiously. Names, characters, and places are products of the author's imagination.

First edition printed in the United Kingdom 2025.

A CIP catalogue record of this book is available from the British Library.

ISBN (Paperback): 978-1-7396167-2-4
Imprint: livelifeyourway
Typeset design: Matthew J Bird

For further information about this book, please contact the author:
http://www.livelifeyourway.co.uk
sally@onehappyplace.co.uk

For everyone living or just surviving their ordinary, extraordinary, life…

Main Characters

Sam – Youngest son
Dan – Sam's older brother
Mike – Sam's dad
Maggie – Sam's mum
Maisy – Sam's girlfriend
Shaun – Sam's best friend
Jody – Maisy's friend
Cassie – Mike's friend

Part I

"Dead Discoveries"
2018, 2019, 1969

2018 – Jody

Life has improved for me.

I moved north from Oxford to a village in the Peak District over two years ago because of Dad's job, well that was the official story, and I started at the local college in September of the same year, I was sixteen. Maisy from my old school has been my best friend since we first met aged 11, but the distance between us means I've made some new friends, initially from the swimming group, now I'm closer to the riding girls. I love being at the stables with the horses, we meet up to ride at least three times a week.

Riding a horse and driving a car are similar, they're both lethal weapons you steer to control. I've surprised myself with how easy I found them to learn because I wasn't great at school. I'm studying to work with animals, spending one day a week at the vets, helping out for the experience. I struggle with too much pressure, it makes me anxious, but I can ride and I can drive, and when it comes to animals I'm so busy focusing on making them better I don't have time to worry about getting things wrong.

Mum and I have all the country gear, gone are Mum's designer blouses, neat little checked skirts and high heels, she lives in jeans and t-shirts and loves her Ariats (fancy boots worn by the horsey community, in case you didn't know, I didn't before we came here) even though she won't go near actual horses. We have become countrified and less worried about presenting ourselves and our house as if we were getting ready for an inspection, which is how Mum was.

The move has completely changed her, in Oxford, she never got involved in anything apart from looking after me and my dad. Here she's joined the local Women's Institute and is on the Village Hall Committee, she decided she wanted a life for herself when I started needing her less and she went out and grabbed it. Half our garden is full of vegetables, some of which we're not allowed to touch because they'll be entered into the local produce show along with her famous baking. I am proud of her, she's ambitious, sometimes without the skills to back it up but you wouldn't bet against her when she puts her mind to something.

Dad adjusted slowly to his new style wife, I could see him processing the changes, raising his eyebrows more amused than cross when his tea was patiently waiting in the fridge for him to microwave, with Mum out at another of her meetings. We regularly exchanged puzzled glances that first year as she pinned up leaflets on our overflowing notice board with some local event or other requiring her attendance, or when we came home to find another friend sitting in the kitchen drinking tea or wine with their muddy boots still on.

His job is amazing and he's been promoted since we've been here. He's the lead project manager for a building contractor. I didn't understand what that was until he took me with him to a "bring your daughter to work day" and I found out how important he is and what a difference his company is making by developing sustainable housing.

We've found out more about each other since the move, and surface-level polite conversations are less frequent. We used to have to surf neatly over uncomfortable subjects, like a stone skimming the water, bouncing along the top before it sinks, subject closed. Mum has driven these conversations and forced us to open up, when she asks how we feel we try to answer honestly which can take a while. It was awkward at first, but I can talk to Mum and Dad about some personal things now. Dad and I still haven't mentioned my pregnancy, I think that would be a step too far.

Sometimes I try to imagine what my life would be like if I hadn't lost Shaun's baby, and I can't picture a version of me with a child. I look at girls who are a similar age to me with children and I know I don't want that responsibility for a long time. I've grown up in the last few years.

People talk of sliding door moments where your life is completely altered based on one decision or a random event, missing a train and meeting your future husband on the next, or your car breaking down and finding your wife with her lover in an out-of-town café you've called at to wait for the recovery services. Events that move us forwards, backwards, and sideways, as if we are pieces in a giant board game. I wonder how much control we have over our lives.

I'm relieved we are finally buying the house we've rented since we moved here. Mum says she can't live anywhere else and I don't want to move again, it's perfect for me, the riding stables are only a ten-minute walk away. The village is the sort you see on a detective series like Miss Marple or Midsummer Murders, Mum used to watch the daytime repeats and I watched them with her if I was off school. The crimes always happened within a three-mile radius, in reality nobody would ever want to live there. Anyway, no crime here so far, but plenty of outdoor types who don't care what car you drive or how many toilets are in your house.

Mum, Dad and I are busy with our lives and grateful for the village and the community who have welcomed us here. This house is the same size as the one we had in Oxford, but Mum isn't constantly cleaning it. She's relaxed and doesn't polish our shoes the second we walk through the door, or clear away our cups the instant we put them down, we've all relaxed.

We get together for Sunday lunch at the local pub most weeks, they serve enormous Yorkshire puddings and bizarrely a side order of fruit, usually sliced pineapple or kiwi with every meal, which makes us laugh. We have loads to talk about and they treat me as an equal most of the time and I like being with them. I've stopped feeling like "Poor Jody," I purposely left that role hundreds of miles down the motorway.

2018 – Maisy

It's the first time I've been home since I started uni, working out the trains was freaking me out and as I get on the train, I realise I hardly ever do anything on my own. I'm either with Sam, the girls I live with or other uni friends hitting the gym, or I'm at their flat for pre-drinks before we head out to a bar or club.

I've managed to get on a much earlier train as mine has been cancelled, I was here over an hour early, I don't know how people can be last minute. The train goes straight from Newcastle to Oxford so I should be there in four hours. I'm so busy with new places and people, it's exhausting and exciting, and as the train sets off, I wonder if Mum and Anna will think I've changed and if being at home will feel the same as it always did.

I spend the journey with my head down, music on, not wanting to make eye contact or have a forced conversation with a stranger. As the train pulls in, I have mixed feelings about coming back to my old home. I've been distracted for a few months, totally absorbed in my new life, and guilt starts making its way into my thoughts to spoil my mood.

I think through Sam's plan for where we might live next year. Sam and I have talked about it, and I think it will work to live with his friend James. None of us has much cash left after rent, food, and laundry. James' parents are buying a house as an investment for him to live in for the rest of his time at uni. They saw his student accommodation and went to the estate agents on the same visit.

James says we can move in with him on the rent we pay now, which will be much better than sharing a bathroom with loads of people. Living apart from Sam for the first year was a good idea, but we're together most of the time doing the same nursing degree, and in the evenings, so we're practically living together anyway. Next year we're on placement and our shifts are likely to be different so we'll see less of one another, but I want to come home to him.

I haven't managed to get hold of Mum to let her know I need picking up early, she's not answering her phone so I'm going to get the bus and surprise her. Sam's coming home next week but I wanted to get back to help Mum with the Christmas shopping.

Sitting on the top of the bus as it drives through the busy streets of Oxford, it feels like I'm a tourist experiencing Christmas here for the first time. Buskers are on every other street corner, food stalls line the pavements, the smells compete as they drift upwards and colourful lights twinkle above and below me. It's getting dark, and the illuminations make it a magical place to be, I am living in a Christmas card.

We used to play a game on the bus called "Spot the Tourist," original title I know. I wonder if I look like I don't belong and we would have picked me out as an outsider, probably, although the inside of me has changed more than the outside.

I can't believe how quickly I've adapted to living in Newcastle, walking through the city every day it's my home now, being responsible for patients at the hospital, actual human beings who think I know what I'm doing, it's another life. I've travelled miles mentally and physically in the last few months.

As I get off the bus guilt takes centre stage again because I've not thought much about my family in Oxford recently. I put my key in the front door and a buzzy excitement kicks in, like having your first drink before a night out, I am pleased to be here. The house is quiet which is unusual, so I head upstairs to drop my case in my room, nothing in here has changed, it's like I've never been away. As I sit on the bed with my feet up, I think I can hear Mum's muffled voice from her room, but I can't make out what she's saying.

I get up, walk across the landing and open her door to find Dad lying naked on top of her. His bare black bottom is suspended in mid-air and his left buttock is showing its faded '80s tattoo, it's supposed to be a red heart with an arrow through it, a tribute to some old band, as it's aged it looks like a plate of red jelly's being stabbed.

They freeze and I freeze, and then I slam the door shut, hoping to erase from my memory an image no child wants to see, the image of their parents having sex.

Five minutes later, after a shouty conversation between them in Mum's room, we are sitting in the kitchen. Mum is red-faced in her modest dressing gown and Dad is unapologetically strutting around in his Simpsons boxer shorts.

I am briefly embarrassed and slightly amused but manage to keep my face straight, as Mum explains,

"We've decided to get back together. Dad is moving in, which I was going to tell you when I picked you up from the station."

She continues,

"Anna is at the park with Ruth, she helps me with her on a Friday afternoon." It transpires this is not a one-off, it has become a regular date in Mum and Dad's calendar since I moved out.

They look happy, so I am happy, and we hug tightly then I stand on Dad's feet, and he twirls me around the kitchen humming "Don't worry be Happy," like he did before he left us. I am instantly transported from the independent young woman I thought I was when I walked in, to his little "Sunshine Girl" once more.

I look at Mum and tears are forming in the corner of her eyes, I think she's been worried about my reaction to the news about her and Dad, she can't believe her story can have a happy ending for everyone.

With warm mince pies in our hands, we watch "Love Actually" where Hugh Grant and Martine McCutchen fall in love, I've done this with Mum every year at Christmas since Dad left. It's a familiar and comforting ritual and signifies the start of Christmas.

When Ruth and Anna join us, we squash up on the sofa, after Anna has squealed at me and flapped her arms wildly mimicking fairy wings, my sister has missed me. It's good to be home with my crazy family.

2018 – Mike

It wasn't entering his clean and tidy bedroom or his neatly made bed that reduced me to tears when Sam left, it was the following morning when I opened the mug cupboard and saw the gaps, giving me tangible evidence another person was missing from this house. Sam and I had become a capable team and the realisation that this once bustling family house now echoes with the sound of only me, gives me the push I need to make some tough decisions, in the new year I will make a new start.

I can't live the rest of my life waiting for the boys to come and visit, putting my life on temporary hold for them. And Maggie is everywhere, it's comforting and heartbreaking, constantly looking at and living a life we should have been living together. Instead, she's at Greenacres, the nursing home, gradually declining with the devastating diagnosis of early-onset Alzheimer's.

I pick up my computer and go online to look at houses, the price suggested for our home is surprising in a positive way, it will allow me a vast choice of property and a plethora of new areas to choose from. I want to live differently, to shake things up a bit. I don't know quite how, I've been existing for a few years and want to be excited by something, this step feels like the right one and I phone the estate agent to come and value our house before I lose my nerve.

My mood continues the next morning when I'm back in the office for the last day before the Christmas break. I realise I am predictable, dependable, boring Mike. When I was Maggie's Mike her brightness shone through me, it infiltrated my soul and lit me from the inside, she made me better and more confident, but now my brightness has faded leaving me wondering who I am. My purpose for doing this job was Maggie and the boys and as I look around the room and register the familiar faces at yet another staff meeting, I know my working life cannot solely be made up of this place, it's not enough. I am unfulfilled, dying a slow death, flailing around, being strangled to conform, suffocating, contained in this restrictive box, waiting for my pension, a bit dramatic but accurate. I am a baby bird wanting to fly.

My thoughts rattle around disarming, disturbing and exciting me in equal measure, they are taking flight. I have no idea what is being talked about in this meeting. The realisation I can do whatever I want, and I'm free to go anywhere is too distracting, it's intoxicating. I can be anything and reinvent everything.

I will start by changing my house and then think about my job, one step at a time.

I want to leave the meeting and explore new career paths but have no idea what else I could do. The old Mike holds me back, keeps me accountable and stops me from being inappropriate and impulsive. I manage to make it until the end of the day before I phone Cassie to see what she thinks.

2018 – Jody

I've been internet dating for months, there's no one I like at college, one guy from the riding group is lush but he's taken, so I've joined a couple of sites. Some close friends have too and we're constantly comparing notes. We start off hopeful, they initially sound compatible and interested, it's addictive thinking this could be something. Then you imagine meeting them and taking it further until you realise you are one of many people they're talking to, but you rationalise it, make excuses for them, persuade yourself they will want you when they know you better, then they stop talking to you for no reason, so you spend your time obsessively reviewing your messages, wondering what you said to get ghosted again. I'm getting smarter at seeing red flags earlier, sticking to my deal breakers and trusting my instincts, and I've stopped believing they lost their phone, their battery was dead, or they had no signal, so that's progress.

My profile picture is quite serious, I don't want to attract loads of interest for the wrong reasons or receive pictures of their anatomy when I'm not going "there" unless I like the rest of them, why would that be attractive?

Unbelievably the guy I'm talking to currently is from Oxford, and he seems to like me. We get on well and chat every day, I'm trying not to get excited, but he makes me smile. I've been here before and met guys who looked nothing like their picture, then spent the date working out how to leave as early as possible, trying not to be rude in the process. I don't know why I'm so polite and I'm not sure why they do it, it wastes everyone's time and you'd be starting your relationship with a lie.

It's like a version of catfishing –

"Look how I used to be, how young and attractive, I know you'll want to date the old me, unfortunately, I can't bring them along because they don't exist anymore." I don't get why you would do this to anyone or put yourself through the humiliation.

I'm going to stay with Maisy for three nights over Christmas and I plan to spend most of my time with Maisy and Sam, they'll be home from uni for the Christmas break, but I've arranged to meet my date for lunch on the last day before I drive home late afternoon. It's a long drive but I'm confident on motorways, they're easier than the single-track roads around here, it's terrifying if traffic is coming around a blind bend, and everyone drives too fast.

Now I've passed my driving test the freedom to be able to get myself anywhere is fantastic and I passed first time, finally an exam I could do. Mum is not so quietly panicking about me driving the long distance, but she's helpfully distracted by being responsible for planning the Women's Institute Christmas party and is frantically speaking to everyone she knows to get the raffle prizes donated.

I set off for Oxford as shards of bright winter sunshine poke out from between the trees. My breath is briefly visible, like an instant cloud, when I shout goodbye to Dad. He's standing in the doorway, with a stream of steam rising from his coffee, surrounded by an impressive Christmas garland, embellished with dried oranges, cloves and red baubles, Mum made it at the local garden centre.

She's becoming proficient at lots of crafts. Art class means we have her pictures stuck on the fridge while she decides if she likes them or not, which is amusing and annoying, most of mine weren't allowed to be on the fridge in the last house because they made the kitchen look untidy, how the rules have changed in a couple of years.

As I drive, I zone out, automatically rewinding to what happened in the final months before we left Oxford. I replay uncomfortable scenes and try to rationalise my thoughts; I know the things people will remember about me and what they will say.

"Pregnant schoolgirl who lost the baby, and a few weeks later moved up north, she ran away."

I think of my sheltered naive little life back then, and how it belongs to another Jody. I don't have much patience for her, who was she, with her small goals focused on one boy for years, wasting her time and expecting good things to land her way.

I smile at my life now and the things I have achieved, grateful for the house move, it might not have happened, if that set of circumstances hadn't occurred.

I can't wait to see Maisy and Sam. Maisy has been over to stay with us a handful of times and I've been up to Newcastle to see them, but it's the first time since I left that we'll all be in Oxford and I'm getting jittery.

When I get closer to Maisy's mum's house the butterflies start, and the anxiety I regularly felt when I was at school here shows up, like the unwelcome old friend you can't shake off no matter how many times you try. I work through some positive reinforcement techniques I've learnt from the internet, tapping various body parts and repeating my positive phrases to the car mirror as I pull in and park. I breathe deeply before I get out, in for four, hold for six, out for eight until I'm a bit dizzy.

When I trap the belt to my coat in the driver's door I almost crumble and climb back into my safe space, cocooned in my car, then I turn and see Maisy, well I hear her first. She has the biggest smile on her face, she is yelling, laughing and skip-running towards me, we collide in a huge hug, and she prances around, reindeer style, not caring who sees us, it's like we're 11 again in the playground.

Maisy is always the same unaffected exceptional friend, delighted by everything, solid and secure with a close circle of friends and family and an inner strength that's in her DNA. Whatever she feels is written all over her face as she chats and bounces with excitement.

Her mum and dad are at home to greet us, and when I see them hand in hand it's hard to believe for a big part of her childhood, they weren't together. Anna, her cute little sister, has grown, she's very smiley despite her challenges, Maisy says she's content, life looks easier for them.

They want to know about me, and I enjoy the limelight, feeling successful for once. I'm never judged here they're genuine people who care for me. Her mum says she misses the cake my mum used to send home with Maisy and asks about my parents and the village we live in.

Maisy and I shamelessly gossip after the polite conversation has ended, we are itching to get out of the house and into town so we can catch up properly.

We spend two nights visiting the clubs we couldn't get into when I lived here, as well as revisiting the pubs we did get into back then, not much has changed.

On night three we decide to have a quieter night to give our livers a rest and meet Sam for a meal at the local Italian. The three of us manage to find out every detail about my lunch date from the internet, poking around in his profiles trying not to act like stalkers, convincing ourselves this is what everyone does.

The next morning, I get ready for my date under Maisy's close supervision, as she straightens my hair, I'm starting to feel like I've never left. A weird homesickness washes over me for a person, not a place, and I hug her tightly, I don't want to leave her.

She tells me not to cry, "You'll ruin your make-up," always the practical parent, she'll make a fantastic mum one day, and she cries enough tears for two.

I drive to the outskirts of town to an ultra-fashionable gastro-dining pub I've never been to, but I've read the reviews on Trip Advisor. I'm hoping "The Riverside" meets its 4.8* rating.

I'm sure it's him because he drives a white Mini, it's on his Facebook page. Ryan gets out as I get out and I know immediately we are going to get on, when he walks over smiling and gives me a big hug.

He looks better than his online photo, he's tall and broad with close-cropped dark brown hair, and his eyelashes are longer and thicker than mine. It's hard not to stare into his perfect dark chocolate eyes. I can feel his muscles through his shirt, it's the sort of shirt confident men wear, pale pink with colourful flowers and tight short sleeves to show off his muscles, his jeans are dark and tight too. I inhale his aftershave as he pulls me into him in a protective way, I could get used to this. He is hot, I am not in his league.

We don't stop talking and lunch turns into afternoon, then early evening, it's easy being with him I can't believe today is our first meeting. We cover random topics, and I know his opinions on a wide range of subjects. I love that he has strong views and believes in things, he's certain in the way he sees the world. He talks a lot, which is good, it gives me less chance to embarrass myself and plenty of time to enjoy looking at him.

A photo of Maisy and Sam pops up on my phone, they are in town for a Christmas night out with Sam's dad, brother and Maisy's mum and dad. I show him the photo and we talk about our close friends; everything's easy and natural with him. It's great to be out and not drinking, I'm in control, and less likely to say something stupid. I know I need to drive home soon, it's a long way and getting dark, I didn't want to leave this late but I'm having fun. When does this ever happen to me? Never, so I'm grabbing the opportunity to spend as much time with him as possible.

Ryan and I agree on a date and time to meet again, and I try to act more casual than I feel when he walks me to my car. He kisses me with force, as I lean against the driver's door, and I stand there for ages with Ryan holding me tight. The kisses keep coming and I'm not going to say no. His hands start to move over my clothing, working their way down my body slowly until they reach in between my legs. He pulls up my dress and knows exactly where he's aiming for, it's exhilarating as he keeps his fingers moving over my G-string, teasing me through the lace before he puts his fingers inside. I move as he moves and the rhythm we create is primal, it's like we've practised this before.

I have a brief panic when I wonder if anyone can see us, and I ask if he thinks there are cameras in the car park. He says, "That's what makes it exciting and dangerous," so we carry on.

When he rubs his body against mine, his finale, I breathe out and a ripple of pleasure riots inside me. I relax into him, and we stand there as I unzip his jeans and make sure he's as happy as I am.

It's around 8 o'clock when I leave, and the heavy rain has just started.

My wipers will not go fast enough for the speed of the battering rain. I drive slowly, concentrating on the road, with my head buzzing with possibilities about a future with Ryan. The sat nav on my car is taking me the quickest route, half an hour into the journey I'm not sure that's the best option, it's taking me down single-track roads and I can't work out how to change it while I'm driving.

I daren't stop, it's dark and there are no streetlights, there's nowhere to pull over. Anxiety begins to rise in my chest as the rain is joined by cracking thunder, and the lightning lights up the sky in front of my car. I turn the music up and try to focus on the words, singing along loudly with Taylor Swift to Love Story.

Driving slowly around a tight bend I hit a torrent of deep water across the road, it's cascading downhill from an overflow pipe. I am too far into the water to stop or reverse and the road is narrow and winding, I can't turn around. I am almost out the other side when my dashboard lights flicker and my car cuts out completely, everything switches off. Frantically I keep trying to start the engine willing it to work, pumping the accelerator, but nothing is happening. I'm wearing a short red velvet dress and strappy high heels, my coat is in the boot, and I am going to have to get out and wade through the water which looks at least knee-deep. Any calm feelings I had are replaced by fear and my learned self-help techniques haven't prepared me for this, I howl and swear, banging the steering wheel with my fists, until common sense kicks in. I can hear Mum's voice shouting, an authority in my head, fighting through the panic, it's organised and sensible, and she's directing me to get out of the car now.

I wade through the rising water, retrieving my coat from the boot and climb up a bank towards the nearest field using the torch from my phone to guide me. I nearly jump out of my skin when I hear heavy breathing, until I realise, I am at a gate next to a field full of inquisitive cows. I try to talk to them soothingly, telling them I am a friend, talking to them as if they can respond. They seem friendly, sheltering under the trees at the edge of the field with me. Then my brain goes into overdrive as it tries to remember the rules where you should and shouldn't stand when it's lightning.

I'm shivering, soaked and alone but my phone is working.

"I am logical and not hopeless, I am capable." I repeat this part aloud, try to feel it, and scroll quickly through my contacts reviewing my options. I guess I'm 45 minutes from the gastropub so ideally, I need to get hold of someone in Oxford, it's far closer than home, Mum and Dad would take hours to get me from here.

Maisy and Sam are drinking in town, so my options are limited. I scroll up again, and Shaun's name stands out. I saw him briefly after moving, he was visiting Sam in Newcastle the weekend I was visiting Maisy. We didn't speak except to say hi, he was with another guy. Shaun is the nearest person I know, will he help me, probably yes. I dial and wait.

He sounds surprised and sleepy when he answers like he's just woken up and he repeats my name slowly sounding out the two syllables as if he's learning how to say it, "Jooo Deeee." I am the last person he would expect to hear from.

It's hard to hear with the rain hammering down, I'm screaming into the phone, trying to explain where I am, giving him the name of the pub I passed, hoping he can come and find me. I look at my car blocking the road, I can't move it, I'm safer standing here, nothing except a tractor or a 4x4 will get through the water, it's still rising.

I wait and wait and sing to the cows and shiver and wait until headlights appear. The car stops and I hear Shaun's deep voice shouting across at me. I say goodbye to the cows and offer a silent prayer to the universe for keeping me safe, then wade back through the water to reach his mum's car.

His mum's given him a flask of tea, some cake and a Waitrose carrier bag containing a pair of her jogging bottoms, a jumper, a coat and thick walking socks for me to change into. I take off my heels and climb into the backseat to swap clothes. Shaun looks out of his side window, away from the rear-view mirror, as I try to get out of my soaking dress. I don't care if he sees me, I hope he's not thinking I have any interest left in him. I stopped caring what he thought and worrying how he saw me ages ago.

I join him in the front seat, grateful and smiling, he's thrown by my confidence. It feels good. I chat, and he nods, no change there then. The freedom to say whatever I want is liberating and I talk non-stop, it's the first time we've had a conversation since I left. I make sure he knows how fulfilled my life is and I'm not falling over my words as I talk about my hot date, he keeps nodding and driving towards his mum's house where we're staying the night. The awkwardness has gone, at least from my side, and our lives have moved miles from where we left them.

I recognise the old Shaun when he pulls into the drive and says,

"My mum doesn't know what happened between us," highlighting the words "between us" by slowing down his speech to emphasise the message and looking at me to confirm I understand. When he asks me not to say anything, I know he's talking about the pregnancy without him having to say the words. As if I would.

Shaun's mum is kind in an efficient and practical sort of way, she's not maternal and doesn't fuss over me like a lot of mums would. Before I shower, I phone Mum, and after her initial shock, when she knows I'm safe, she asks a hundred questions about what happened and where I am. She's coming to pick me up early in the morning and she'll phone the insurance company so they can move my car. I am calm and composed when we speak on the phone, like a duck sailing along the water but with my legs paddling frantically under the surface. I am the actress version of Jody in this house.

I put on a pair of Shaun's mum's pyjamas, they are green striped and full length, functional not flirty, and I start to feel self-conscious when I walk downstairs to join them in their sparse lounge. Nothing in this room is welcoming.

His mum tries to chat and asks me where we live now and how my day was before I drove into the water. I don't want to give any details, it's uncomfortable discussing my new life and my hot date, with Shaun studying his feet and his mum sitting there in the audience, it's like being interviewed.

"Have you got any new hobbies?"

You can tell she's not used to making small talk, and we have big awkward gaps in conversation when no one knows what to say. Shaun is exactly the same as his mum, smart and silent. They are trying not to be rude but I'm not interesting enough for them, their worlds revolve around academic ability, it's their measure of success, and my animal world is of no interest to them. Her questioning is turning me into another version of myself, usually, I can talk about anything with anyone, but now I can't think of a single worthwhile thing to say, so I ask if it's ok to go to bed, and I can see I'm not the only one relieved the conversation is over.

I study the bathroom when brushing my teeth with a new toothbrush and unfamiliar toothpaste, and I wonder in what decade a burgundy bathroom was fashionable.

Once safely in their spare room, surrounded by various widths and shades of green stripes on the curtains, walls, bed and pyjamas, I text Maisy and Ryan to tell them where I am. Maisy doesn't reply, I guess she's still out. Ryan sounds concerned and says he can't wait to see me, we keep texting for over an hour until I fall asleep.

Breakfast is the same uncomfortable ordeal as last night, sitting at the dining room table with a mismatched teapot, toast rack, and butter dish, and a jar of half-empty marmalade placed between us with crumbs and bits in. I don't think they're used to having guests. Shaun looks like he's been gaming all night and was forced to get up, managing to answer me in five words when I ask him about his uni degree.

The doorbell rings and Shaun's mum jumps to answer it, as if her life depends on getting to the front door in record time. We quickly follow her to escape a further conversation, you can almost hear the room breathe out as everyone leaves, flooded with relief like the rest of us that the torture is over.

Mum is standing there with her politely fixed smile, the one she saves for people she doesn't like, and flowers for my host as if she's coming for dinner not rescuing her daughter from the boy who broke her heart. She declines an offer to come in, Dad is waiting in the car, and a formal exchange takes place on the doorstep, with one daughter swapped for a bunch of lilies and roses.

Shaun says "hello" from the safe distance of the hall and Mum gives him one of her looks, she's conflicted because he's rescued me, but he badly damaged me before. His eyes involuntarily blink with panic, he's wondering what she might say next, but it's uneventful. Mum and I say thank you and as their door closes, I know part of my life remains firmly shut, trapped in a time I have successfully chosen to forget.

2019 – Cassie

Mike and I are not together romantically, we're just friends, that's what we tell each other, which is difficult for me as I've been in love with him for a few years. In every way except being intimate and sleeping together, we behave like a couple. Every week we go out for food, we usually have a long walk and end up at a pub somewhere, eating and drinking more calories than we've burned off, convincing ourselves otherwise. I call at his house several times a week, and we phone and message every day.

We are comfortable in the other's space; we can talk about anything and are open and honest, almost. Mike and I are supportive, an exclusive team of two. We are opinionated conspirators when we become amateur food and wine reviewers, taking on ridiculous characters with obnoxious viewpoints, and finishing our private observations in fits of giggles. We act like children who've had too much sugar, giddy and occasionally inappropriate like an over-enthusiastic dog finally let out for a walk. I miss him when we're apart. It's a revelation to me that I can be me with somebody else, flaws and all, and be accepted, it's got to be enough for now. It won't be enough forever. I know this type of relationship can exist and I want this, I want to be the most important person in somebody's life.

Mike has become less self-conscious when we go out, it was uncomfortable for him, being out in public with another woman after Maggie, even as friends, he cares a lot more about what people think than I do. I've worked with so many patients and relatives, counselling them at the worst time in their lives, helping them to find a path through to a future they can live with, some still worry about judgement from other people, most desperately want to do the right thing. I've learnt over the years, you can't please everyone and you'll kill yourself trying, so go with what you think is right, the guilt will be there whatever you decide.

I like helping out and enjoy cooking for the boys at Mike's when they're home, I think they appreciate the home-cooked food, he loves it when they're back, they are a tribe of three. I never feel left out though, they know how to include me in the conversation. They are a credit to their mum and dad. I'm looking forward to catching up and finding out how Sam and Maisy's first term studying nursing has gone. I'm not sure what my role is or what they think of me, I hope they see me as their friend.

Maggie is doing well at Greenacres she settled in from the start. She chose to go there before Alzheimer's took her decisions, selflessly trying to make it easier for her family, living there permanently is what she wanted. I helped them all at the start, counselling and listening mainly, it was tough, Sam was 16 when he found out. Mike and I visit her together sometimes, he holds her hand if she'll let him, his love for her will always be there.

2019 – Sam

Cassie answers Dad's phone in the kitchen because he has his hands full. He's putting the roast chicken in the middle of the table completing our roast dinner. She follows him in, and we can see from her face it's not good news. She's telling the caller to slow down and keeps saying,

"Ok, ok, ok, they are setting off now."

Cassie looks across at the three of us about to sit at the table for lunch, and as calmly as she can, using her professional counselling voice, tells us Mum has been hit by a car and we need to go to the hospital now.

She ushers Dad, Dan and me out of the front door then Dan takes over, getting into the driver's seat with Dad beside him and me in the back. The hospital is 15 minutes away if there's no traffic. Dad phones

Greenacres on the way to find out what happened. The manager says the new receptionist and one of the temporary carers didn't stop Mum from leaving, they thought she was a visitor. Dan and I can't hear much, but we watch Dad shaking his head. Apparently, she walked straight past them in the reception area then ran outside, down the steps and into the path of one of the resident's daughters' cars. She was reversing out of the car park after visiting her dad. Mum and the daughter have been taken to hospital; they don't know much more than that.

On the way to hospital every possible scenario plays out in my mind as questions push their way in. What if she dies? What if she's paralysed? Where will she live? Will she be taken to a normal hospital ward because she has Alzheimer's? Will they know how to look after her properly?

Dad is in shock, quietly processing, it's how he is, he'll be trying to protect us by working out how to deal with it and what to say, creating a safety barrier around me and Dan.

We've been lucky, Mum loves Greenacres and we all know it's her home now, but Mum in a hospital, how will that work?

After trying to park for over 10 minutes we decide to abandon the car and run in. We're directed to a private room and when we walk in, Mum is asleep, heavily sedated. When the car hit her, it broke her right leg and she hit her head as she fell, it's not life-threatening.

The nurse is calming, professional and reassuring when she delivers this news. Her approach is a lesson for me in how to do this with my future patients.

We sit at the side of her bed, three ducks in a row, feathers ruffled, with Dad in the middle. Raising our eyebrows, breathing out, dropping our shoulders, anything to let out the tension, side smiling and shaking our heads at each other. Even though she hasn't known who we are for a long time we know we need to be here for her and for us.

The daughter who hit her knocks gently on the door and lets herself in. Tears are streaming down her face, and she's struggling to speak, she's apologising over and over again saying,

"I didn't see her; it was pouring with rain when I started reversing. She must have run behind me and seconds later there was a deafening bang. I got out and she was on the floor, she didn't scream or cry she just looked lost."

We are trying to comfort Emily, the daughter, when Mum opens her eyes and looks suspiciously at the four of us, narrowing her eyes and frowning. She leans across and over to our side of the bed, between the bed frame and our shoes, and is violently sick on the vinyl floor. It breaks the tension as we swiftly move our feet.

"Get out now!" Mum screams.

Another nurse arrives and we wait in the corridor, before being sent home a few hours later. As we leave Mum is speaking loudly and asking where she is and why she isn't at Greenacres. She's disturbing everyone, shouting for her clothes, we know it's as normal as she's going to get. Thankfully there's no long-term damage from the accident, the damage has already been done when Alzheimer's took her from us.

The drive home has a carnival atmosphere, I guess this is how it is when you win the lottery, instead of prize money, Mum's life was the prize. It's the type of life we don't want for her, but we don't want her not to exist either. It's hard to think about, she's still our mum, and dad's wife, according to their marriage certificate anyway.

Dad jokes about how tough she is, and we talk about her before the diagnosis, we don't often do this the three of us. We cover the hole she leaves with paper, it's easy to get in, but it's still emotional to replay what we've lost. He continues talking, he's in a jubilant mood, listing our childhood illnesses and any hospital visits, trying to remember which one of us broke their toe and who had a septic knee, Mum would have known.

As we pull into the drive Dan and I exchange glances, like some secret code, we know how lucky we were to grow up with her abundant love, she was fierce the way she loved us, she was the lioness, and we were her cubs.

The next part of the evening is surreal, we've time travelled back into lunchtime, sitting in the same places we always used to sit when we lived here, except Dad sits in Mum's chair when Cassie is here and she sits in Dad's, I'm not sure if this is an intentional move. We are starving and poised to eat as we pick up a conversation from hours ago.

"The best part of a roast dinner I think is the gravy" Cassie continues, and the friendly debate starts up again.

Cassie puts the now cold chicken in the middle of the table near the reheated veg and hot gravy. Dan and I stab for the crispiest roast potato, which in my opinion is the best bit, and Dad decides this is the moment to tell us he is going to sell the house.

Before I left for uni, I would have stormed off to my room and caused a scene with news like this, now two things cross my mind, firstly I am starving and need to eat and secondly, it might not be a terrible idea.

Cassie looks down at her plate, uncomfortably involved in our family drama, as Dan asks if he's moving house on his own. I know from his delivery Dad has rehearsed his answers, practised them like an actor would run lines, he was anticipating objections and for once they're not from me.

"I am moving alone to a three-bedroomed apartment in a serviced block with a view of the river, a swimming pool in the basement and a gym on-site in case I want to use it. There are shops and pubs within walking distance." He smiles when he delivers this speech, selling it to us with a confidence I don't think he feels.

He deflects the attention away from the decision and tries to involve us in a debate.

"How do you get a corner sofa into an apartment; do you think we can take the window out or get it over the balcony and through the double doors."

I play along like the supportive son I am trying to be and offer help if he needs it.

"The gym and pool will be cool; can we all use it? If so, I'll come home constantly?" I joke.

Dan and Cassie are noticeably quiet.

2019 – Dan

Sitting in the loft isn't the way I would choose to spend my Saturday afternoon, but I've promised to help Dad sort the house out before he moves. I've got time, I'm not back at uni for weeks and it's the final year after my degree. I decided I wanted to become a teacher so I'm mainly on placement experiencing what Mum must have gone through at my age. I wish I could talk to her, and she could reassure me I'm getting it right, some days I don't feel in control of a class of eight-year-olds. They gang up against trainee teachers it's like they can smell my nerves a mile off, like the giant in Jack and the Beanstalk. My day consists of a constant stream of children taking toilet breaks, the whole class is never in the same place at the same time.

It's taken a while for it to sink in, he's actually going to move. I don't want Dad to move, the reassurance of him being here is comforting and familiar, it's hard not to feel like we're leaving Mum behind. I can see he's becoming a new person, and I know it's good for him, changing and growing, discovering a life for himself beyond us, I'm happy for him as long as he doesn't change too much.

I open a cardboard box, the size you would put an average cat in to go the vets, it's marked Mum's stuff, and inside I find two smaller boxes sitting side by side. I think they might have been from my gran's things when she died, they look like they haven't been opened for years.

Inside the first box, I look at a row of numbered envelopes neatly lined up in what appears to be date order from front to back, according to the ones with postmarks. I don't recognise the stamps, the writing on the envelopes is beautiful, neat, precise, and written in a formal style no one would use now, not that anyone I know writes letters. It looks like three or four different people's handwriting, there's one in a heavier black pen and a curlier artistic style written in a dark blue. There are nine in total including one that has never been opened, it's marked "Return To Sender" in big letters.

I carefully pick up the first envelope and remove the letter, the paper is thin, I start to read. I am intruding on private, intimate lives, but I can't stop now.

What I discover transports me to another place, a crueller one, with heartbreak, disappointment and fear jumping off the pages, I am holding my family history in my hands. I can't stop reading, it's like a film playing out in front of my eyes, my poor gran left alone and abandoned, her life was nothing like I thought it was. I'd never considered her early life when she was a girl herself, she was just my gran.

As I wade through history, it seems important to respect the letters and the secrets they hold. Questions float randomly in my head, and I try to make sense of what I'm reading, I need to share this with someone, to talk it through, to see if it means what I think it might mean.

I lie flat on my stomach and shout through the loft hatch aiming my face at the stairs.

"Dad, you need to see this, urgently."

"Give me a minute and I'll come up; do you want tea?"

Five minutes later we sit huddled comfortably between the rafters and he tells me about the last time he was sitting up here, reading Mum's old diaries and learning about her life before she met him.

He picks up letter number one and starts reading.

2019 – Mike and Dan

The first letter has no address on the envelope, it says "Carole" which was Maggie's mum's name. It has a hand-drawn heart in the top right corner where the stamp would usually be.

I open it and read what Dan has read, re-reading the loving words twice to make sure I'm taking in the correct details.

Letter number One

July 19th, 1969

My beautiful English Rose,

Well, well, well, I came to visit my uncle in Oxford, and I met the girl of my dreams, that's why I love this crazy world, you never know where it might take you next. Carole, you are everything to me. Do you believe in love at first sight, I didn't but I sure do now. We live in different countries but how we think and what we believe makes me realise our values have nothing to do with where we grow up, they are fundamentally embedded into who we are, I am rambling on, sorry, I don't seem to be able to stop talking!

I can't sleep, waiting to see you again, I don't want to sleep. I keep thinking of you looking devastatingly beautiful in your bright blue dress when we first met at the village dance, you were as pretty as a picture, smiling across at me. Your smile gave me all the courage I needed to walk over and take your hand in mine and lead you onto the dance floor. The slow number was a masterstroke, I got to hold you close from the beginning "This Guy's in Love with You" will always be our song.

I feel like I have woken up from a dream, no, a nightmare that was my life before you came along. I have never known such joy, and the happiness I feel when I think about you after knowing you for just over a week is ridiculous! My heart is jumping around in my chest, be still my beating heart!

I don't want you to worry, we will work everything out, I want to spend the rest of my life with you, and I know you feel the same, love always finds a way. Now I've found you, I won't let you go. I promise I'll look after you, cherish you and be back here to sweep you off your feet as soon as I can.

I didn't want to wait until I got home to write, I wanted to leave a part of me behind in this letter so if you have any doubts, you can read exactly how I feel to remind yourself of my love for you before we can be together again.

Love always,

Your American Hero (your words not mine!),

John xx

Letter number Two

July 22nd, 1969

My beautiful English Rose,

I am writing to you from the plane, we have just left each other, and I feel a hole opening up inside my heart where you should be, here next to me. It is a physical ache, I am lovesick without you and already planning my return to England before I land back in the US.

The distance between us won't change anything, be strong my darling Carole until we are together again. Look at the stars and remember we are under the same sky, I will find the brightest star and stand on the porch every evening looking up at it, thinking of you. The light you have brought into my life shines inside me, I want to be a better man because of you, and my mission is to see you again as soon as I can.

I have included the chocolate wrapper from the aeroplane, I'm sorry I couldn't send the chocolate. I know you are curious about the type of chocolate you get on board, be reassured, it didn't match up to the fancy type you make at the factory, and I told the stewardess this!

I hope you have started eating more now, my appetite is returning, I'm like a hungry horse, nothing normally stops me from eating. I will post this from the airport when I land, please write soon so I know you are well and hopelessly in love like me!

Love always,

Your American Hero,

John xx

Letter number Three

30th July 1969

Dear John,

My very own American Hero,

Thank you for your letters I will cherish your words forever, we fit together like puzzle pieces as you would say. I never knew love would feel like this, and I felt the same as you did at the dance when you took my hand, I wanted you to hold onto me forever.

I cried in my room after you had left. Mother noticed my eyes were red, but she didn't ask why, she knows about the time we spent together so she probably guessed you had gone home, she would never speak about it. She treats me like a child, and we cannot talk about anything personal.

The girls at work noticed I was smiling and made me tell them all about you. I told them how we first met at the dance and how we walked for miles in the park with your arm protectively around my shoulders. They said I blushed when I mentioned being huddled under your umbrella before we stopped for our first kiss in the rain. How the hours disappeared when I was with you, it was like we'd known each other for many years. They laughed when I said we had stayed up all night just talking, most of them are older than me and already married, I can't believe they ever felt this way.

I don't know much about America apart from what you have told me, but it sounds tremendous. Your world is very different to the one I live in, and my job is so boring compared to yours, flying high in the sky and saving us all! I am surprised you chose me out of all those girls, I want to be with you wherever that may be, I am so proud to be your girl. It feels like a dream to me too, everything has happened so quickly. I've never spoken to anyone this way, but it is how we talk when we are together, I hope it is alright to speak like this. You have given me the confidence to tell you how I feel, I wonder if all Americans are as confident as you.

I felt like the luckiest girl in the world when you gave me the red roses, you are spoiling me, be careful I might get used to it! No one has ever bought me flowers before, I have put them in my room on the windowsill, a secret signal of our love for passers-by to admire, and I can see them from my bed, I will press them to keep forever when they start to wilt. Mother didn't mention them, I don't think anyone has ever bought her roses and I wonder if she's jealous.

I have nothing exciting to tell you, nothing has happened here, but don't worry I have started eating again. I live every day waiting to hear from you, checking the post and hoping something arrives, giddy, and excited about our future. Some days I want to burst with happiness to dance and sing and tell the whole world how magical our love is, other days I don't want to talk about us and taint our love by sharing it with the world outside my heart. I don't want to hear other people's opinions, so I keep my thoughts to myself, safely sheltering my feelings, and protecting us.

I am desperate to see you again, a part of me left with you, write soon my love.

Your English Rose,

Carole xx

Letter number Four

August 8th, 1969

My beautiful English Rose,

Your letter spoke straight to my heart, my dearest Carole, I love you. I can't stop smiling when I think of you and the future we can create together.

I need to ask you something, I think you know what it is. I want you to move to America, to come here and live with me, to be my wife. I wish I was there to get down on one knee and do things properly, but I can't wait until I see you again, I need to know you are mine. Our time apart is painful for me, and I can propose formally when we next meet, I will make sure you'll get plenty of red roses with my proposal!

I think I know what you will say and once I know for sure we can start making plans and decide where we want to get married, and if you are happy to, you can move in with me and Laurie. The ranch is big so we won't get in each other's way, I know you will love her, and she will adore you. You can decorate our rooms however you like, bringing your English style and charm to make it feel like your home. I go to sleep every night imagining you here beside me and I feel like the luckiest man in the world, I am not sure what I did to deserve you, but I promise I will love and cherish you for the rest of my life.

I hope we will have children, at least two, a boy and a girl, but I am getting ahead of myself! Did I mention we have a dog? I hope you like dogs, I don't think we talked about pets. I will stop rambling and wait impatiently for your reply.

Love always,

Your American Hero,

John xx

Letter number Five

18th August 1969

Dear John,

My very own American Hero,

Yes, Yes, Yes!

It is the easiest decision I have ever made. I want to spend my life with you, wherever you are I want to be there. I would be honoured to become your wife. How long do you think everything will take to organise and do we need a special licence because we are from different countries? There is so much to sort out as we plan the rest of our lives, I am overjoyed and overwhelmed to be your fiancée, our love has happened so quickly.

It will be a little frightening leaving everyone and all that is familiar, but I know you will take good care of me, and we will support each other. I am not sure how to tell my mother, you have to pick your moment with her, and I haven't found the right time yet. I must warn you I am not a great cook, but I am capable of running a house in every other way. I hope Laurie likes me and doesn't think I am too young. I worry she might have preferred you to marry an American girl so they had more in common. I am looking forward to meeting her, it must be such a beautiful bond being a twin. I can't imagine what it must have been like growing up so close to your sister, going through life with someone to talk to, it must be comforting to have never felt alone.

I have felt quite alone for a lot of my life, particularly throughout my childhood, I was unable to easily share how I felt, regularly changing who I was to try to fit in and play with the other children at school. No friends came home, and I wasn't allowed to play outside, it was what the common children did. I have friends at work, but I am never comfortable revealing too much about myself, words can be used as weapons, and I've always been frightened of being vulnerable and getting hurt. I suppose I never fully trusted anyone, that was until you arrived, how you've changed me and brought me to life. I want people to see me now.

I look in the mirror and see the same face with its polite existence reflecting at me smiling, inside the shy quiet person I was is finally being heard and I want to tell you everything. I was behaving the way my mother sees the world, she trades in others' misery and delights in their misfortune, but I am learning wonderful things can happen, I cannot wait to leave her opinions behind.

I am like a rose, your rose, opening in the summertime, finding my perfect time to bloom in the garden, you have given me the confidence to show myself, you make me feel beautiful, you make me believe I can do anything, be anything and go anywhere, I love you.

Your English Rose and wife-to-be,

Carole xx

Letter number Six

August 27th, 1969

My beautiful English Rose,

I received your letter, and you have made me the happiest man alive. We are going to be husband and wife and grow old together. I have never wanted anything more than I want to be with you.

Please don't worry about Laurie she loves all things English, and she will love you. We are close to our English uncle so I think we can claim to be a little bit English ourselves when it suits us, you will fit right in here I promise.

I have a test flight booked for next week so I will be away for maybe a month. They are developing something new, it's top secret and they want me to run the trial flights. I am going to a little airfield in the middle of nowhere, I haven't flown from there before. It will be excellent to take to the skies and look down on the world again. We are "the birds of the air!" I miss flying regularly, it's the only time I feel truly free, swooping around in the clouds, but I would swap it in a heartbeat if I could spend an hour with you.

I will look at everything paperwork-wise when I get back, and I'll arrange some dates to visit you very soon, after all, I need to meet your mother. We can spend the time planning the sort of wedding you would like when I visit, I don't care about the details as long as we're legally married, and I can carry you over the threshold back here to start our married life.

I will write you a longer letter about my adventures in the skies and tell you about America and what a magnificent country it is after the mission. I hope there will be a letter waiting for me on my return, I will look forward to it.

Love always,

Your American Hero and husband-to-be!

John xx

Dan

Letter number seven is the one that appears to have never been opened, marked across the front with the words "Return to Sender." The sender's address, Carole's, is on the back. It's on the back of all the letters she wrote. I presume this was a standard thing to do years ago. I'm trying to see if it was ever opened and resealed, it wasn't.

I'm holding a letter my gran sent to America 50 years ago which was returned to her for some reason. I feel uncomfortable opening it and pause to look around the loft, seeking approval from the boxes surrounding me, before glancing at Dad who's still concentrating on an earlier letter.

I gently put my little finger into the corner of the envelope, it opens easily, it's the shortest letter so far…

Letter number Seven

1st October 1969

Dear John,

My very own American Hero,

I didn't want to write until I was sure and now I am. I know you have been away, but I need to speak to you urgently, it has been difficult not talking to you. Please can you arrange to visit or call me soon? I have news I cannot share with anyone but you, please get in touch. I love and miss you and I desperately need you. I think it will be good news but it's a bit sudden and I am in shock. I hope you won't be cross I don't think so, my head is all over the place and my heart is bursting with love, I need to hear from you. I think you might have guessed what I am going to say.

Your English Rose and wife-to-be,

Carole xx

Letter number Eight

October 13th, 1969

Dear Carole,

I am sorry to have to inform you that John has been killed on a routine test flight, he died on September 27th.

I know you were making plans to be together, when he came back from England, he talked about you nonstop. The only comfort I can take from his death is he was doing something he loved.

I am sending the last letter you sent to him back to you unopened, it didn't feel right for me to open it. Forgive me, I am struggling with my grief and cannot write much. I have lost my brother and my best friend, and I understand you too have lost someone special in your life.

I am truly sorry.

Kind Regards,

Laurie Gray

Dan

It takes me a minute to process that the postmark on the envelope of the letter from Laurie, has a date on it a few days after the postmark on the envelope of the "Return To Sender" letter. This means Carole's letter came back first, unopened, so she didn't know he had died.

As I breathe out, I say, "Dad he's dead."

The last letter looks different from the rest, "Carole" is handwritten across the front, in heavy black capital letters, taking up a third of the space on the envelope, the letters are bolt upright and look cross.

Letter number Nine

22nd October 1969

Carole,

I have decided to write everything down to help you understand what you need to do next after the mess you have got yourself into.

I can't speak to you in person because you won't listen, but you need to stop crying and take responsibility for what you have done.

You have two choices, you can either have the baby adopted. I can find somewhere for you to go while you have it and no one will know, then you can carry on with your life. The other option is to get married now, to make this baby acceptable to our family and friends it needs to be born to married parents so you would need to find someone who wants to marry you. Before you say anything, I am sure you will have more children when you are married, and the time is right.

Any other choice you make will not be acceptable and you will not be welcome at home, you will be on your own. I know this may sound harsh, but it is for your own good, you will understand one day when you are a mother yourself.

Whatever has happened to him, the American, and let's face it we don't know for sure, despite what his sister has said, it is evident he is not going to be here to help you, so you need to move on from him.

I do not wish to speak to you about this at length, but I will need to know what you decide so I can make the necessary arrangements. I am disappointed I have to write this letter, I thought I had instilled in you better values; however, I know we will move on from this God willing.

Mother.

Dan

As Dad is reading the last letter, I open the second small box with trepidation. Inside is a selection of old random items with no value to anyone except my gran, to her, I imagine they would have been the most precious things in her life.

I pick out a blue silk hair ribbon embroidered with tiny white flowers and rub it between my fingers. Then carefully lift out some fragile pressed faded roses that look like they were once red, I place them on my palm to show Dad. A ticket to the local village dance in 1969 follows the roses out of the box. It has an image of a couple twisting on the front, it gives us the date Carole first met John on Friday the 11th of July 1969.

Underneath the ticket is a black and white photograph of a tall handsome man, looking confident and proud, in what I presume is an American Air Force uniform. A folded white serviette with "My English Rose" written on one side and encased in kisses comes out next, and squashed flat at the bottom of the box is a milk chocolate wrapper with an aeroplane logo on the front.

Small mementos, quietly hidden away from the rest of us, everyday items loaded with meaning, lying there peacefully for years, betraying the impact they've had on Carole. They are the catalyst for everything that followed.

I raise my head, exhausted from the depth of emotion that's been stirred up inside me. Dad looks shocked, we hug tightly. It's an intense snapshot in time, the dates of the letters from start to finish cover less than four months but they were life-changing months, true love found and lost and what they reveal changes our family history completely.

Part 2

"Learning Lessons"
2019, 1969, 1970

2019 – Shaun

As I crash into the parked cars my cock is in Ady's mouth, and it doesn't take a genius to work out we are in big trouble. The back of Ady's head hits the steering column as the front of Mum's Golf crunches into the side of a smart black Audi. He sits up dazed, and a trickle of blood starts to leak through his bleached blonde hair as I zip my jeans up. We are less than two miles from where we set off.

It's 1am on a quiet street in the suburbs of Newcastle, or it was until we arrived. House lights are turning on and curtains are twitching, doors begin to open and the noise from the car alarms is deafening. A range of dishevelled people arrive in various items of nightwear, outfits randomly thrown together that were not expecting a public outing.

Concern for our safety is the overwhelming sentiment from everyone. Ady obligingly plays along for the crowd, enjoying the attention and being at the centre of everything, while they dab gently at his head. This is the moment I know our relationship, if you can call it that, is over. In the Bible, this would be when the scales fall from my eyes. I realise nothing will ever be about me; it will always be the Ady show. It's not that he's a bad person but he is a caricature of himself. He lives his career choice, life is a performance, but when you dig deeper and scrape through his façade there's little left inside him that's real. He's disappointing and I wonder if I need to tell him I don't want to see him, I'll probably let it drift, it will end itself.

Conversations are rife up and down the street like this is daytime, the growing crowd fills their time by catching up with the latest gossip before the police arrive. They are huddled in tight familiar groups, young mums and dads, middle-aged neighbours, pensioners, and teenagers. They are obliging extras, playing their part in our drama, listening to one another but paying attention to the soap opera in front of them not wanting to miss anything, it's like Eastenders if it was set in Newcastle. This will be all over Facebook and Insta by now, we will be local celebrities. I observe how quickly it appears normal for them to stand outside chatting in the middle of the night and wonder why they consciously stay and freeze.

The Audi driver runs towards me in short paisley pyjamas and matching slippers, she's got an orange tan and heavily Botoxed lips. She stops to inspect her car and returns inside to fetch a torch to spotlight the damage for us all to see. She starts to cry dramatically, sobbing about how long it took her to save up for her dream car, I look away.

Two police cars arrive, and any brief sympathy the crowd felt for me disappears as I blow into the tube, everyone knows I am guilty of something.

"Step inside the car please young man."

He's only a few years older than me and delivers this line smugly, like he's been doing the job for years, speaking politely in a monotone voice from the '80s, as if he's auditioning for a role on TV. It comes with a strong local accent, I think he's enjoying his job too much, I bet his family are proud.

He waves across at a young group and his face says, don't worry, I'm in charge now, no need to panic. Bollocks I'm in big trouble, I obediently climb in.

Ady does his best to look surprised at the outcome of the breath test, shrugging his shoulders, his traumatised face is sickening. Then he tries to distance himself from me as if we were travelling together by accident, casual acquaintances not lovers, as he speaks to the police. I'm looking forward to cutting him out of my future.

We've been together for three months, he's the opposite of me that's why I liked him, outgoing, popular, spontaneous, he's what I thought I wanted. Great sex and no ties, it's not a relationship, in a way I have been paying him for sex. He's never bought me a drink, paid for food, paid for anything. He'll move on to the next person tomorrow and I will be choosier next time, not blinded by the shiny outside and flattered by the attention.

Maisy tried hard to disguise her dislike of him, I think her opinion softened slightly because she found him funny, he disarms you with his humour. Sam looked at me with his "really" face as he let us out of his flat earlier this evening, staring disappointedly at me and shaking his head. He asked us to stay the night, and I might have, until Ady convinced me to drive the car to the hotel promising hot tub action later.

As Ady danced down the street to some disco tune in his head, prancing in and out of parked cars like "My Little Pony," complete with jazz hands, I convinced myself that driving was perfectly acceptable.

Reality hits me like a brick when we enter the police station, like a swift well-aimed kick in my guts, it's as if I have been physically assaulted. We went on a school trip to a police station when I was about 12 and had a tour, someone's Dad from my year worked there. We had a rare day out and role-played what happened to an arrested man, from booking him in, to holding him in a cell. Then when we were back at school we went through a full trial and pretended to be the criminals, the police, the judge, and the jury, ironically, I played a policeman, and we did a project on it. Sam got a headteacher award for his poster "Don't end up in a cell, live well!"

Mum is going to kill me, but not yet, she's in Greece for a couple of weeks at a yoga retreat. She's in the mountains somewhere, I can't even remember the area, so I'm going to have to phone Dad.

When Dad walks in he looks like the capable lawyer he is, despite the time, he's dressed smartly for the occasion. It's nearly light outside as he walks past me and Ady across to the reception desk, almost ignoring us.

He has a conversation with the young policeman, and I can see his shoulders lifting and his head nodding from the back, Dad is in charge, he's on familiar ground, this is his home turf.

When he eventually turns to face me, he raises his eyebrows and puffs out his cheeks trying to get control of himself by blowing out the build-up of carbon dioxide. I see the surprise planted on his face, he's like a deer caught in a trap, wanting to be anywhere except here. I'm not sure if he's surprised because Ady's holding my hand, or because I've done something this idiotic, probably both. He doesn't speak and I don't want to meet his eyes, so my eyes dart everywhere except to his face, they land on Ady's trainers, I study his colourful laces with contempt. I owe Dad an explanation, maybe multiple explanations, but I want to be alone with him before the shouting and disappointment begin.

We walk to the car and Ady jumps on the spot with childlike excitement when he sees Dad's red Porsche, I am starting to hate Ady. I stare at him to make him stop but he's oblivious to his inappropriate behaviour and he continues to make loud hooting noises to match the manic jumping. I let Ady sit in the front, it's like treating a child to the ride-on car at the supermarket. I squeeze into the back seat that's not made for real people to sit in.

Ady lists all his favourite cars on the way to the hotel, it's a long list, including Ferraris and Lamborghinis he'll never own, I have inadvertently crossed "to ride in a Porsche" off Ady's bucket list. Dad to his credit silently nods, he's as irritated as I am. It's how he behaves when he's dealing with a client he doesn't want to represent, you wouldn't know he didn't like you from his actions unless you knew him well. Ady and I collect our things from the hotel room in silence, the hot tub sits unused.

Dad says I need to stay with him to sort out Mum's car, he knows I've had enough of Ady. I thought Dad didn't know me after he left us, we argued more than we talked, dialogue was a constant battle. I was always point-scoring for a quick win, it was easy because he made some stupid mistakes, three wives for a start, maybe he knows me better than I think.

We drop Ady at the train station after Dad buys him a ticket home to Oxford. Ady doesn't thank him, he frowns at me then pouts and whines because "I should know he doesn't like to travel on his own."

Dad is having none of it, his steely determination turns the atmosphere cold, and he leaves Ady no alternative, so he gets on the train before Dad's patience runs out. Then he phones Mum's insurance company from the car to deal with the aftermath of my mess. We don't have the music on, and we don't talk, I'm waiting for him to make the next move, it's like we're playing chess.

Dad's tone is matter-of-fact as if he's reporting on the weather when he speaks, we're approximately halfway into the journey.

He says, "Shaun can I ask you something?"

"Yes"

"Are you gay?"

"Yes"

"Ok, I wish I'd been the sort of Dad you could have shared that with."

And the conversation I've worried about having for six years is over. Endless practices and the varied scenarios I'd run through in my head never ended this way. I didn't predict this conversation; I've wasted unnecessary time wrongly judging his reaction.

He looks at me to see if I'm going to say anymore, I don't, and he doesn't, immediately my life feels lighter.

It takes the rest of the journey for the conversation to sink in, as I get out of the car in Oxford I'm struggling to work out where my dad has gone, the one who's so wrapped up in himself that he doesn't leave space for anyone else.

2019 - Sam

The first time I met James we were standing in line, freezing, waiting to sign up for the uni football team. It was the beginning of September, and he had a Newcastle beanie hat on, a grey washed-out tracksuit and old trainers, he looked like he could have been sofa surfing. He was the least likely person to come from an affluent background with rich parents from the way he came across. He asked me where I was from and what I was studying, and we swapped bite-sized portions from our past and immediately hit it off.

We've started going to the pub after football practice for a debrief, we both enjoy the challenge of training but don't take it too seriously, unlike some of our teammates who we discuss at length over our pints. Our friendship is relaxed, James is easy to get on with and it's good to have someone to talk to apart from Maisy.

He invited me to his family home a few months later when he was going back for the weekend. He's less than an hour from uni, near Durham, to say his background was a surprise is an understatement. He'd given me no insight into the sort of life he lived before coming here. When he talked about his mum and dad, he said he got on well with them and I said the same about my parents, translating the bare facts about my mum being at Greenacres.

As James drives into the gated development, he stops to put his code into their private gate post, and it strikes me that we don't know much about each other's home life. The gates swing open, and I try to remember which film I feel like I'm in as we drive down a short lane through the middle of an orchard full of apple and pear trees in neat lines on either side. He doesn't speak and I don't know what to say, I manage to say "Wow!" my English teacher would be proud.

The lane bends to the left and standing majestically before us is a huge three-storey white house with perfect grounds. The trees are elevated and manicured into the shape of birds at the top, with beautiful gardens everywhere you look. The greenest grass is manicured within an inch of its life like it's waiting to be judged. It reminds me of a scene from Alice in Wonderland the whole thing is immaculate. I compare this to my mum's garden with her chaotic planting and haphazard colours and smile at the contrast. There are no wooden swings with paint peeling or tatty treehouses here, it's a garden for show not to play in, Mum would have loved to see this.

The car crunches on a deep layer of gravel as we park beside a limestone wall in front of the house. He doesn't say anything until I mention how massive the grounds are, to James this is normal. Then he explains his mum is quite a well-known gardener and they sometimes film here for television.

We walk into a large hallway with the biggest staircase up the middle I have ever seen in real life, there are doors in every direction. Murphy the black labrador greets us enthusiastically and I follow James to the kitchen, it's the first room on our tour of the ground floor. The downstairs toilet has a bidet and side-by-side sinks, it's the same size as our dining room in Oxford. The house is impressive with two entire floors decorated similarly with marble flooring, white paint, glass and silver furnishings. Everything is modern and matching, designed by someone who knew what they were doing. It's like walking into a magazine set and nothing like the home I grew up in.

We head up to the top of the house with Murphy following, it turns out James has the third floor to himself. His bedroom is at one end, the lounge is in the middle and his bathroom is at the other end. It's not an attic, it's a full floor of the house, like an apartment with a balcony out from his lounge overlooking the garden. You can tell it's his space, it's a boy's den, tastefully done, painted in blues and greens with comfy leather sofas and a massive TV on the wall, I'm instantly comfortable up here.

He can see how shocked I am, internally I'm trying to stop the adjustment that is unfairly taking place within me about who James is and how far apart our lives are. His bedroom is at least six times the size of mine and it has a pool table in it. We drop our bags and start to play, from the first break we could be in any pub, and our friendly banter returns as we concentrate and compete, desperate to beat one another. I win, sport is a healthy leveller, James suggests we go to the local pub so he can buy the victor a pint.

We jog downstairs and I have an overwhelming urge to slide down the banister. I restrain myself, thankfully, as his mum comes in with Waitrose shopping bags when we arrive at the ground floor.

James is a carbon copy of her with identical blue eyes, an open smile and a hooked nose. They are both almost six feet tall, with athletically toned bodies and tanned skin that spends it's time outside and is used to holidays in sunny places. She hugs us and is genuinely pleased to see me; I can't believe I'm staying here for the weekend.

At the pub, it's a welcoming committee, everyone knows James and is happy to see him. I guess when you grow up in a close community, attend a small school with 25 pupils and your social life takes place in the one pub or at the village hall, you are bound to know everyone. James explains as we are part way through pint number four, that's why he wanted to move away, to see how he would survive on his own, he wanted to live like every other student for the first year at least. He says he didn't want me to see him differently, but didn't want me to think he was hiding anything, that's why he brought me home.

I'm honoured he trusted me enough to share his life before uni. His mum is famous locally, and people keep asking about her. I have no idea who she is. He says she still uses her maiden name for television work, so he can easily remain anonymous out of the area with his surname, and he says she's not that famous unless you're into gardening.

After pint number five we walk up the lane to his house and sit in the kitchen with his mum, helping ourselves to chilli and garlic bread. They call it supper, I call it tea, either way, it tastes brilliant after the beer. We chat as I relax and talk about Maisy and my nursing degree, his mum is interested, and I briefly mention my mum and dad, feeling at ease enough to share some of my history. I'm surprised at my voice; I sound like I'm reporting on events that happened to someone else, I'm speaking in a detached and informative way. I keep talking and practice telling my story to this captive audience ignoring the counselling nods and concerned eyes. I make it through what I wanted to say, and his mum passes me a whisky and hugs me, it's not awkward except I don't drink whisky.

On Saturday James and I go for a walk that lasts all day. He takes me on a tour of where he grew up, made dens, had his first kiss, and more. We walk by the river at the bottom of their land and swing across it on a tyre which I'm not sure is safe, but I chance it anyway. The pub features again for lunch, and we bond over their homemade steak and ale pie, chips, peas and gravy.

When we get back his dad is home, and predictably, he's friendly, chatty and seems kind. He's been golfing and won a trophy, he jokes with James how easy it is being a student, then offers him money if he needs it.

We leave early on Sunday, I feel like I've been away for a week, the break is what I needed but I'm ready to see Maisy and show her the photos, she won't believe the size of his house.

As James drops me off, he says,

"If you ever want to talk, you know where I am."
I nod, knowing I could and would, talk to him.

2019 – Shaun

On the way to the airport, Dad glances at me, irritated, his mouth is twisting with displeasure, and his disappointed face has returned. He looks displaced sitting in the driver's seat of Mum's car, and we all know his time is money, this isn't where he expected to be on a Wednesday afternoon. I am legally allowed to drive until my court date, but Dad's not taking any chances, he won't let me near Mum's car.

In the two weeks since I crashed, he's been behaving in the way I presume normal Dads are supposed to behave, supportive and caring after he loudly got the message across that my behaviour was not ok. He sorted everything out car-wise, the damage wasn't that bad. I'm waiting for a court date, Dad thinks I'll lose my license and get a massive fine. He makes the point repeatedly,

"If you had injured someone you could have gone to prison."

But I didn't so he doesn't need to keep going on about it and I've found out it won't affect my law degree thank God.

I see Mum before she sees me as she walks through arrivals, she's chatting to the person next to her and looks relaxed until she sees Dad standing next to me. Her demeanour changes instantly and her amble becomes a march, taking ankles out with her suitcase in the process, pushing past everyone to get to me. She stands in front of us, hands on hips and Dad tells her not to panic which has the opposite result, he always manages to wind her up with the minimum of words. I think she expected the effects of the yoga retreat to last longer than the return airport.

The journey home is a replica of one from my childhood, sitting in the back, not speaking, feeling alone, hoping the shouting would stop. Distracting myself by looking into other car windows and deciding which family I wanted to be teleported into, mentally leaving this one. I always chose one with a boy about my age, figuring if the new parents didn't work out at least we'd have each other. Sometimes, if I really liked him, I'd smile and half-wave. All my adultness has been left at the airport, I am powerless, it's as if I am not here. I'm the luggage going round and round on the conveyor belt, waiting to be collected, wanting to get off and be taken home with new more competent owners.

Mum doesn't speak directly to me until we get into the house. She has vented to Dad and made it abundantly clear this wouldn't have happened if he had been here for me when I was growing up. Personally, I don't think it would have made any difference, it's not only children from single-parent families who get things wrong. Mum is still blaming him for the way her life turned out, so the ammunition is useful, she's peppered him with insults and I can't blame him for leaving straightaway.

She doesn't know how to punish me, she can't do anything unless it's financial, she can't ground me I don't live here. I say what she wants to hear, "I'm sorry, I was an idiot, and I will never do it again." When she believes I mean it her ranting stops, it's a game we've played for years, like two cats marking their territory until one backs down, that's me. She says it was a shock, something terrible could have happened to me, and I know part of her rage is because she loves me. I can't wait to get home to uni to live my real life.

I am two people, a child at home and an adult at uni, slotting into my old life is impossibly uncomfortable. I need the freedom my new life gives me away from the way I am supposed to behave. Dad understands I need my space, he's been fighting for his since I was born, but Mum doesn't get it.

I can see she's hurt when I say I'm thinking of heading off tomorrow, I can't stand the guilt. Living my old life makes me smaller, I'm squashing myself in. She's trying to fold me up into her neatly packaged son, it's like trying to cram the cardboard into the recycling bin when the lid won't shut, I don't fit in here anymore.

2019 – Maisy

As Kai closes his eyes for the last time, I close my eyes too, and every part of me begins to question if I can do this type of work and become a nurse. This will be my reality if I become a children's nurse, coping with a revolving door of death, yes, lots of children survive and get to go home but some die. I know this sounds obvious and it is, however, the reality of dealing with life and death on a ward is a long way from the classroom theory, it's like reading how to swim and then jumping into the channel to swim to France.

This is my first death on the children's ward, and I sit very still with my head in my hands, as my tears spill out, I have no power to stop them.

I jump when his mum pulls back the flimsy curtain and falls to the floor when she sees me crying and knows he's died. She went to the toilet for less than five minutes and in that time, Kai has gone somewhere, or nowhere at all, I don't know. I do know he's never going to open his eyes and smile at his mum again, she will never hear his voice, his babyish laugh, and his demands for chocolate buttons.

When his mum gets onto the bed and lies beside him to hold his still-warm little body close to her for the last time, I go and find someone who will know what to do. She would have given her life for him; I think I might have given mine too. Kai lived for four short years, how does that make any sense, it's not right and the impact of his death is making me question my whole life. His imprint is stamped deep within me, there's a type of grief and a lack of comprehension raging about I've never felt before. I feel trapped in my body and I'm not sure how to deal with it as the world cruelly moves on, seemingly unchanged, oblivious to the destruction of one boy's life.

Systems and processes leap into action seamlessly, this is new to me, but the team are professional and compassionate in death, they've seen it many times. People move around me being useful, but I can't move. The time of death is recorded, I managed to remember to look at my watch, and as one family experience the worst outcome for their child, I am stunned into a silence of injustice. I thought I was prepared for nursing; I've been looking after Mum and Anna for years. Everyone said I'd make a brilliant nurse, and I presumed I would, I never imagined the pain I would feel when a child didn't make it.

When I get home, I am physically aching, and I try to explain the impact of Kai's death to Sam. He quietly listens and says everything I should need to hear. He is logical and rational, but I can't stand the textbook answers on how to cope with grief when my recurring emotion is guilt. Sam does his best to answer my questions as I get frustrated with the indiscrimination of death.

"Why was I the last person to see him alive?" I took that away from his mum, she should have been there.

"Why didn't I know what was happening and run to find her?"

"But if I had run to find her, he might have been alone when he died and that would have been worse, wouldn't it?" I don't know what to think.

Every time I stop and try to think and process what happened, Kai's peaceful face appears resting on his pillow. He flashes up before my eyes, it's so real and I keep looking at his face, really looking, studying him for signs of pain, willing his eyes to open one last time for his mum, it's like we're still in the same room. Then I see his foot out of the side of the bed, and I remember how many times I've tickled it, and tucked his perfect little foot back into bed over the past few months.

He had dark curly hair and dark brown eyes with long eyelashes curling upwards, he was a beautiful child. Kai loved racing up and down the corridor on a shiny red fire engine, he took his cuddly Piglet for rides in the truck and always wore Winnie the Pooh pyjamas. He was a bit wild, but we let him get away with it, even when he tried to run us over, he giggled and squealed when we pretended to tell him off, he knew how to get us to do what he wanted.

His mum nearly lived here and knew the ward and the staff better than I did. She was warm and friendly and kept thanking me for looking after him, saying how kind we were and how much he liked being here. A couple of times she apologised,

"I'm sorry I smell of smoke, I stopped smoking before he was born, I know it's a reckless thing to do but it's helping me cope."

Each time I smiled at her, maybe I should have said something.

You could see she was constantly worried, with purplish black circles under her eyes and clothes now two sizes too big, she was visibly disappearing. Whenever we checked on Kai through the night, she was awake, I don't think she's slept properly for months. I think she is the bravest person I have ever met and she's making me question if I am cut out to be a parent.

I suggest to Sam that we go out later. I need to blank out this desperately empty lonely feeling, I am coming unstuck. I've been found out. I don't measure up and ultimately, perhaps I can't do this as a job.

The first drink goes down fast but it's soothing like medicine, ironic, I know. We have five or six vodka and cokes at home, measures unknown, and head out to the 2-for-1 bar in town. After two more rounds, we queue for the club, I am trying to stand upright and lean into Sam for support. If I look drunk, I won't get through the door, and we have to get in because I need to dance.

Sam is trying to persuade me to leave and go home, but I'm on a mission to block out today and stop thinking about anything hospital-related. His voice seems far away and irrelevant, I can't be bothered to respond to him. I know he won't leave me here alone, and he reluctantly guides me through crowds, into the dark loud space with blinding strobe lights shooting above us. Once inside I leave Sam and take my place in the centre of the room dancing to Abba's "Dancing Queen" with my arms up, shouting the words and stomping to the music, I have left my inhibitions at the door, and it feels fantastic.

Sam is watching me cautiously from the sidelines, he's irritating me by being Mr Sensible tonight when I want to let go. I pull him across to dance with me, he's so boring, I release him quickly and have fun spinning on my own. I join a group of three boys, and they whirl me around their circle, I move from one to another laughing and screeching like I'm on the waltzes at the fair.

I leave the dancing group, and we wave and blow kisses, it's easy to make new friends when you're drunk. I sway towards the bar, pushing past people to get a drink, it feels important to keep drinking. I've lost sight of Sam and I don't care. I prop my elbows on the wet metal surface and try to shake the sticky liquid off my arms. It's like a switch has been flicked on, and I'm suddenly aware I feel dizzy and extremely sick. I blindly stagger towards where I think the toilets might be, desperately trying to remember which direction to walk in while my legs threaten to give way, disconnected from the rest of me. I look down the stairs and miss the top step, that's where my memory of the evening ends.

I wake up for the first time surrounded by strangers dressed as nurses, in the uniform I wear as a student nurse. I can't understand if this situation is real or if I'm dreaming, I am tightly trussed in a hospital bed, stuck in some nightmare, hallucinating about work in my sleep. I sort of recognise someone, but they're blurry, fuzzy at the edges and I can't work out where I know them from. My head won't move from the pillow and the lights are piercing and burning the pupils at the centre of my irises, as they do their job and let the light in, I'd like them to stop.

It's eight hours before I wake up again and it's lunchtime according to the clock opposite my bed. This time I know exactly where I am, the smell is a giveaway, and the nurse in charge of this ward, who is also my mentor, is standing next to my bed telling me I should try to have some lunch, but I'm not hungry. I have no memory of last night and how I got here.

Sam arrives and he fills in the time gaps, apparently, I fell down 15 steps and landed heavily on the tiled floor at the bottom, he's surprised I haven't broken any bones. I arrived by ambulance, and he came with me panicking, flashing blue lights all the way, while the crew looked concerned as they checked my vitals. He says it's different when you love the person who's in trouble, he was behaving like the relatives we reassure, and I was unconscious, like a ragdoll when they picked me up. They put the lights on in the club and switched the music off until they'd wheeled me out, brilliant, so everyone saw me.

I attempt to get up to use the loo and wobble as I try to stand. Sam holds on to my arm to escort me, I am walking like an old woman who needs a walking frame.

When I pull up my hospital gown the superficial bruising has begun to appear alongside some swelling and my body aches when I move. I'm so embarrassed, but they won't let me leave until a doctor agrees to the discharge, because I was unconscious, they want to keep me in and observe me for a few hours in case I have a head injury and a delayed reaction.

I sit miserably in the bathroom on the freezing toilet in the corner of the room, making Sam wait outside the door while the food I've eaten for the past two days runs out of me. I rest my spinning head on the V-shape I make with my hands, my head is too heavy for my neck. The hangover is horrible, I deserve it. It's the worst headache I've ever had, jungle drums are beating loudly on repeat while simultaneously a snow globe is being shaken angrily by my conscience, as my stomach growls and rumbles.

I have never done anything like this before, and I'm mortified people know I'm here in the hospital, the one I'm working at, completely wasting everybody's time when they have real patients to cope with. I'm a waste of resources, time and money, I know it and they know it; they need my bed, and I don't deserve their kindness and care. Hot cross tears explode as if they've been waiting for an occasion to erupt for a while, I would scream at my stupidity if it wouldn't disturb the other patients.

I wonder if I will get kicked off my degree. Sam is chatting and being kind, I know he's cross with me, he wouldn't say it, but I know him. We've talked about self-inflicted patients at uni, and how important it is not to pre-judge anyone, we all have a back story, and you can't know what's happened to drive people to that point. We all nod and say the right things in the lectures but it's hard not to think differently when you compare my thoughtless actions to an innocent child with a genuine need to be here, like Kai, here to be cared for at the end of his life.

We leave the hospital late afternoon and Sam tries to make me feel better, he's bought chocolates and flowers, they're on the back seat, which makes me feel worse. Once home, I shower and change into my favourite pyjamas while Sam prepares my comfort tea, the one I have when I'm not very well or tired. The tomato sausages and mashed potato smothered in gravy sit looking up at me from the plate balanced on my knees, they remind me of Mum and Anna.

I have an appointment booked in two days with the university counsellor before I can start my next shift, which gives me masses of time to stress and worry about my future.

2019 – Sam

After Maisy's unplanned trip to the hospital, we spend the weekend talking about nursing. Kai's death has made her question everything, she's a different Maisy, unsure, hesitant, and full of remorse. I push her with questions to make her talk, I've not experienced a death at work, it's only a matter of time, I don't know if this is normal.

She keeps repeating,

"You don't know what it feels like until you experience it, the sense of helplessness is overwhelming."

I phone Dad and he says I need to listen to help her work through it, and for me to not try to fix it for her. He says she doesn't need me to solve it, she'll need time to process and understand why she reacted the way she did. We have a grown-up chat, and I get the impression he's pleased I phoned and asked for his advice.

I can switch off easier than Maisy can, and leave work at work most of the time. Maybe it's because of my mum, she's always in the back of my mind, but I can't let thoughts of her and Alzheimer's take over my life too. I've learnt how to control my thinking and carefully manoeuvre lightly around the painful bits, so I can enjoy and be present in the rest. It's the same when I visit Greenacres, I drop my negative thoughts at the door and walk in having transformed into the perfect son for the residents, I am my own magic trick.

By Monday Maisy is ready to fight for her nursing career and we've practised what she'll say. We made it light-hearted, role-playing the friends and colleagues we know from home and work, taking on their personalities and impersonating their accents, swapping roles making it appear less serious than it is. She's worried they won't think she's suitable to continue the nursing course, I'm trying to convince her people will have done far worse things than got drunk, and the fact she's so worried means she cares and should absolutely be a nurse.

We've decided being honest about Kai's impact is the only way to explain her behaviour, to make sure they understand how out of character this is. Maisy has more tears at home before she sets off, she thinks they'll be cross and question her ability to become a nurse, she keeps saying she's let everyone down. I think Anna, her sister, is wrapped up in the way she's thinking but she won't talk about her. I know leaving was hard, she'd cared for Anna all her life. In Maisy's head, it's as if talking about Anna will make something bad happen to her which makes no rational sense, but I guess how we feel doesn't have to make sense.

After pacing up and down for an hour I hear her keys in the lock, she bounds through the door all smiley and gives me a bear hug, I lift her off her feet and spin her around. Maisy says they were understanding, not cross just concerned, and have offered her some counselling which they've insisted she attend. She's the first one in our year to go through this experience and apparently, her reaction is quite common, not the hospitalisation part, but questioning your choice of career and needing time to work through it.

We make plans to go home together in the next few weeks. I want to go home for the last time before Dad moves, and I can never go there again. I'm not sure why I need to, I've said goodbye to that life now I'm at uni. The house has the best and the worst of memories. Every room holds a kaleidoscope of experiences, its secrets are imprinted on my brain, with reminders that randomly seep out of me as I re-live what I learnt there in my new world.

Our past lives live in photographs on the walls, undisputable evidence Dan and I should have gone to a proper hairdresser. Shared memories have been re-written, from the easy-going family we were to the barely functioning unit we became before Mum moved to the nursing home.

Sometimes I feel I am an adult, and it's happening more and more, especially at work on the wards, I step comfortably into that role. At other times when big decisions come towards me, I still want to duck away from them and let them fly past. Maisy says she wants to go to Greenacres for the day while we're back. She will be the star attraction at the nursing home, she'll keep Mrs Brown quiet and give them a rest from her barked head teacherly instructions. I want to see Mum and catch up with Bert, one of the old gentlemen who lives there, I still don't know why he's a resident. I like spending time with him, he's always full of words of wisdom and we talk about music.

2019 – Mike

When I phoned Maggie's dad, Reg, it was like he'd been expecting my call, he wasn't surprised to hear from me. He said he has two letters he wants to give me, and he wants to explain, but he's not willing to discuss anything over the phone. He emphasised this in his "I'm the expert in the room" voice.

"A visit is long overdue, it's about time you came to see me in the sunshine so I can put the record straight."

Spoken as if we were friends and communicated regularly.

I wanted to say we've never been invited, but my upbringing jumped in and politely responded.

"We would love to visit; it will be great to catch up."

I felt disloyal to Carole and Maggie as soon as I ended the call, like I should have defended their honour or stood up to him in some way, which I convince myself is unfair, I need to try not to pre-judge. There are two sides to every story, and I want to keep an open mind however much I dislike him.

Six weeks later we are on our way to Spain.

The boys and I chat constantly throughout the flight, discussing all possible outcomes of the visit. I am starting to be more like the boy's friend than their parent, in the last few years they have helped me as much as I have helped them. We talk about my apartment and how excited I am to move when I get back, I can see they've accepted it and seem excited for me.

As the plane touches down at Malaga airport I register that we've never been on holiday the three of us, it has always been us four, Maggie, me, Dan and Sam. I've not had a holiday since Maggie moved to Greenacres full-time, I've not thought about one, I was too busy learning to live my life without her and dealing with the boys. If Dan hadn't opened Maggie's mum's box with the letters in, we definitely wouldn't be here now looking for answers, it's funny how things turn out.

We walk down the steps of the plane and a rush of hot air encircles us, and empty blue skies, blazing sun and another climate greet us. We walk across the tarmac and into the terminal, it's chaos inside, with snaking queues stripping off clothes, revealing white legs and midriffs preparing to turn red.

We make it through passport control eventually, because it takes them a while to believe the little boy photo of Sam in his passport is the same young man standing in front of them after the computer said no.

I feel like that a lot of the time in reverse, with the men in front of me hiding their boy model inside somewhere.

Relief comes in the shape of an air-conditioned limousine-style taxi which drives us to the hotel. I automatically get in next to the driver, who turns out to be from London, temporarily resuming my dad status. Our conversation is like everyone I've ever had when I'm in a city I don't know, so I'm used to playing along.

"You here on holiday?"

"Yes, for a week." I don't want to go into any detail about why I am anywhere, I wish they wouldn't ask.

"Where are you from?"

"Oxford"

"World-class university in Oxford and they're in that boat race."

"Yes"

Sometimes, depending on the genre of television my taxi driver prefers, the conversation moves onto TV and film, and the line "Morse comes from Oxford" regularly makes an appearance. Not this time.

"Have you been to this part of Spain before?"

"No"

"You need to visit Ginos, fifth along from the dolphin fountain on the main street, for the fabulous food if you like fish."

"Thank you, we'll take a look." I have no intention of doing this.

"Club-wise, you want to go to Tropical because it's got the cheapest drinks and opens until 4am."

Me, "Thank you."

I am painfully aware I need to be grateful and enthusiastic, but I can't fake it, I want to discover a place for myself. Maggie and I spent hours exploring, walking the backstreets on holidays, dragging the boys behind us. I prefer the bits the guidebooks don't tell you about, we walked miles trying to find where the locals went to eat, the food was better and cheaper although we weren't always sure what would arrive on our plates, but that was all part of the fun, usually. A whole ink squid and sheep's brains forced us to buy a translation book on one holiday a long time before we had mobile phones, fearing our Oxford stomachs weren't up to this cuisine.

Dan and Sam are not aware of this predictable exchange, they are busy catching up. Thankfully we are not staying far from the airport and the racing speed he's driving at means we arrive in 20 minutes.

At the hotel reception, we are directed to a symmetrical white box, it's a spacious, sparsely decorated family apartment with a wide shallow balcony off the lounge at the rear. We lean over the warm metal and the boys pretend to admire the side view of the baron countryside to make me feel better, while I silently wish I'd paid the extra for the sea view at the front and wonder how much weight the balcony will take as we stand in the welcoming sun. I didn't want to spend the extra money; Maggie would have persuaded me it would be worth it, and she would have been right.

The boys are in high spirits and say they don't intend to spend much time inside. We each put our luggage on a single bed, they want to go out and explore, I want to unpack, I always unpack first, it's what I do. With the realisation that "boring Mike" has reappeared, I inhale calmly twice and counsel my brain to leave the unpacking and we all head to the bar for our first sangria of the holiday. "Mañana!"

The town where Maggie's dad lives, the dad who brought her up anyway, is less than a mile from here and I need to work out what I am going to say to him after little contact for years. I have no idea what's happening in his life, and he doesn't know much about ours.

He knows about Maggie moving into the nursing home permanently because I wrote it in a Christmas card, "Merry Christmas, and in case it's of any interest to you, your daughter's Alzheimer's means we can no longer look after her, so we've had to send her away forever!" I didn't write that, I was brought up to respect my elders although I question that wisdom now, but it's what I felt like writing.

I muse about tomorrow's conversation over a delicious dinner of tapas and sangria, which interestingly we've learnt from the waiter is the Spanish word for blood, at a typically Spanish restaurant on a street parallel to the hotel. As we eat, I look at Dan and Sam and wonder why we haven't done this before, put some distance between everything to give us a chance to adjust to being a family of three. Maybe it's the alcohol but I manage to declare, "I'm so proud of you," and I smile, thinking Maggie would be pleased I'm making progress by telling them.

They respond laughing in unison with the words "We're proud of you too Dad," which nearly sends me over the edge and has me dabbing my eyes with my napkin.

We are happy and relaxed away from our everyday lives, it's like we've left them in our seats on the plane or dropped them into the middle of the ocean, it's special to have the boys here all to myself for a week.

The following morning, I wake up smiling and refreshed, with a positive frame of mind. I think the three of us can tackle anything as we head down to the help-yourself all-inclusive breakfast. It doesn't take long before the seven and nine year-old versions of my sons emerge, disarming me and throwing me back to past holiday memories, as enough food is placed on the table for three times the amount of people sitting there. Pastries feature heavily in their choices and Sam has chocolate milk which contradicts the way he looks on the outside. Dan and I smiled at him queuing at the milk machine, towering tree-like over the other chocolate milk drinkers, oblivious to what was happening around him, he was tuned out.

Breakfast eaten, we wrap the extra food in serviettes for later, in case Spain has a food shortage, pack our swimming bags, and set off on foot for the town.

Maggie's dad runs a small bar and restaurant, it's easy to find on the second corner off the main street because it looks English. It proudly displays its Union Jack bunting across the top and the English breakfast menu stands triangular outside, showing photos of what the food should look like on a good day. Every way to cook eggs is displayed in the pictures and baked beans are present on every image, it could be on an English high street. It stands out shouting amongst the traditional bars, like I remember him shouting in public, embarrassing us all for no reason on numerous occasions.

I can't help thinking Reg will have come to Spain to live like an Englishman without embracing any of the Spanish culture. I'm expecting him to be a visibly older, browner, heavier, possibly balder form of the man I knew.

We are almost at the entrance to the bar when Reg and his wife rush out to greet us, they must have been waiting and watching from inside. Reg firmly shakes our hands in turn, and comments on how much the boys have grown. Then he annoys me by asking which is which, as if they haven't developed their language enough to answer for themselves. His mere existence is irritating, and I don't underestimate his ability to destroy my positive mood.

He looks like a tourist in patterned shorts and a tight white T-shirt which does nothing to hide his expanded stomach, he's wearing yellow sliders, exposing fat hairy chunky chip-shaped toes. He could be featured in one of those saucy old postcards, the ones I hadn't registered were sexist until Cassie and I had an amusing debate. I have never seen him in casual clothes it's disconcerting, I can't compute that this is the same intimidating person I knew in Oxford.

They play the perfect couple and try to feed us from the minute we arrive. In the absence of any meaningful conversation, we talk about food and the Spanish weather. Reg verbally tries to work out how long it has been since he saw his grandsons, counting on his fingers like he's five. I know roughly when it was but don't feel like helping him out, he's not physically been in the same place as them since he left over eight years ago.

If he'd walked past the boys, he wouldn't have known they were blood-related, there is no way he would have recognised them. I start to wonder how many people we must walk past in our lifetime that we are related to. Millions of us are walking through life connected, oblivious to our bloodline.

Barbara his wife heads inside, she disrupts my thoughts when she reappears with a photo album. Despite my best efforts, I can't dislike her even though she's connected to him.

She's the opposite of how Maggie's mum was, she's loud and opinionated, a forceful lady with a sing-song voice that goes up at the end of every sentence, it sounds like she's Australian or always asking questions. She has dyed red hair tied in bunches, worn how a significantly younger woman would wear it. I correct my judgemental thinking, it's not up to me how she wears her hair.

"Call me Babs, everybody does, no one calls me Barbara, it's a serious name, far too serious for me!"

They moved out here the year after Maggie's mum died. Reg had been calling into her little Oxford café for years before they got together, Babs knew him and Maggie's mum well. She must have seen something in him I can't see, the phrase "love is blind" springs to mind.

I think the thing I like about Babs is that she puts Reg in his place. She's not afraid to contradict him and she says what she thinks. She sends him into the kitchen to make me a drink, I've never known him make a cup of tea, so this new Reg will take some time to get used to.

She keeps chatting, "Reg has been nervous and excited about your visit, it's dragged up memories he's buried but not forgotten, and we've had a few tears."

Babs doesn't say this with any blame attached, I don't respond. I have to admit he appears to have mellowed.

The man in front of me, handing me a cup of tea, bears a passing resemblance to the English version I once knew and actively avoided, but I'm cautious, in case the old one chooses to show up. Reg is trying hard to be hospitable, he's playing the attentive and humble host, he wants to please us and demonstrate how successful he is, I wonder if he expects me to applaud.

Personality-wise he's perfectly pleasant, I'm making him sound like a disappointing hotel review "perfectly pleasant but wouldn't stay again 6/10." Appearance-wise he's gained weight and lost all his hair, my guess was right, I try not to be pleased. He brings out the worst in me, Cassie would be telling me people can change, and I should try to be kind, I'll message her later.

The boys are enjoying reconnecting, but I can tell they're getting bored. They're desperate to go across the road to the beach and I want to talk to Reg on my own, so when Babs suggests Reg and I sit around the back where it's quieter the boys take it as their opportunity to leave.

We move to what he tells me is their private garden, and the scent of lavender and rosemary surrounds us with fragrant purple bushes and terracotta pots everywhere. We sit at each side of a small white wrought iron patio table for two, sharing a stripy parasol to shade us from the sun. If I were here with a person I wanted to be with, I would appreciate the beauty of this moment, it's perfectly set up for a photo, a memory to bank, to re-live and enjoy in the future, except for the company.

Babs arrives in an apron and serves us refreshing iced coffees and slices of homemade lemon cake. We sit looking down at the table, clouded in awkward silence for minutes that feel like hours before he says,

"I'm guessing you've come about this?" as he gets a letter out of his pocket.

Reg nods as he passes me a thin blue envelope as if he's permitting me to open it. It has large old-fashioned spidery writing on the front I vaguely recognise. The envelope shows its wear through the years. His face is blank like he's playing poker. It is addressed to Carole at her mum and dad's address. I open the letter and start reading.

Letter number Ten

25th October 1969

Dear Carole,

I am sorry you are upset, and I have considered your predicament after our conversation yesterday. I wanted to let you know I have a suggestion that might work for you and your mother.

I would be willing to marry you but unwilling to inform anyone about your situation and would ask you to do the same. This is to protect myself and your child from prying eyes and the stigma of being conceived out of wedlock. I want us to be like any other normal family, we need to be socially acceptable. There is no reason anyone has to know the baby isn't mine.

You will find I am a stickler for detail, I hope you can cope with that. Although things are not ideal, I think we can make a go of it, and I am willing to support you and bring up your unborn child as my own. As you know I cannot have children due to a childhood illness, so this gives me the chance to become a parent, the arrangement will work for us both.

In time I would like to think we could grow fond of each other and maybe love will grow. I expect your decision tomorrow. I will call around to see you after I have delivered the morning post.

Reg

Reg starts to comment on his letter and where it came from as I'm reading the last few lines, explaining,

"I found two letters in the pocket of Carole's old cardigan after she died. It was hanging at the back of her wardrobe. I didn't know she'd kept my letter, and I can't understand why she wanted to keep it."

I can feel him willing me to read faster, his eyes burning into me, fidgeting in his chair, bursting to speak. He says the way he wrote it seems so formal now.

"I was scared to death, worried about what my parents would say but I loved her, loved them, in my own way, and Carole needed a quick solution to the shame of being unmarried and pregnant and her family put pressure on her you see.

It was harder than I thought, I had no experience with children, but I tried not to resent her when she arrived and came between us like she did. When I first looked into Maggie's eyes, and they weren't like Carole's, I wondered what I'd done marrying Carole when I could have found someone else to love me, moneywise I wasn't badly off. Looking at Maggie she might as well have had a necklace on saying I don't belong to him."

He stops speaking and looks up, trying to engage me to judge my reaction, hoping for some acknowledgement before he ploughs on.

"I was always left out, they had their secret jokes, a separate language, they spoke in code there was no room for me, she didn't need me you see once Maggie arrived, no one knew she wasn't mine, I'd served my purpose, and Carole was obsessed with her. I knew Carole didn't want me, she was way out of my league, she was still in love with a dead man and it's impossible to live up to a dead man who will always be the hero. I was jealous and bitter, we should have got divorced but you didn't back then." This speech tumbles out of him in a rush.

Reg has tears in his eyes, he looks embarrassed, and I'm embarrassed by his vulnerability. He sounds defensive and I watch as pieces of the old Reg start to emerge, he is looking for an ally in me and I am the last person he should ask. Maggie was my wife and his daughter in every way except blood, and I know how hard he made her life when she was growing up. He instilled in her self-doubt and a sense she would never be good enough, Maggie never felt he was proud of her, and now I know why.

I ask if they ever spoke about Maggie's real dad. "We didn't, not after we were married and she was born, I wouldn't have allowed it, and I don't think Carole ever told her the truth."

Reg continues by stating he regrets his behaviour while trying to justify it, re-emphasizing he was young and times were different.

"We didn't talk about everything back then, people weren't constantly examining their feelings, what was done was done and we had to make a go of it, we weren't endlessly searching for happiness it was enough to put food on the table and go on holiday once a year. I know that's not a great way to live, but our expectations were a lot lower then, I'm wiser now I'm with someone who wants me and loves me properly, it was lonely being chained to a woman who could never love me back."

He stops talking and looks me in the eye, he's almost pleading with me to sympathise with him, hoping I will make him feel better. I can't excuse any of his past behaviour, but I can empathise with some of it, however, I will never understand how he could take his frustrations out on a helpless child. I don't want to acknowledge how it was for him, it feels disloyal to Maggie and his negative impact played a part in what she believed about herself for years, so I nod at him and say absolutely nothing, I need some thinking time.

When the boys return from the beach we change the subject, there is nothing left to say as far as I'm concerned.

I can see he's trying to build bridges; he says he wants to know about them and be in their lives in the future. He's asking questions as their grandad that he should have asked years ago. I can't work out if he's showing a genuine interest, maybe. He's waiting for answers and offering no judgement, he always dished out plenty before, Reg was confident he was the authority on every topic. I'm relieved they're grown men capable of making their own decisions regarding an ongoing relationship.

Before we leave Reg gives me another letter with the number eleven on the front of the envelope. It's addressed to John and has never been posted. He asks me not to open it until later.

I put it with number ten safely in my suitcase when we're at the hotel. I'm curious but I don't want to open it yet or mention it to the boys until I know what's inside. I want us to enjoy our holiday and leave the past in the past until we get home, it's time to live in the present.

The rest of our holiday is memorable and I get to experience the type of holiday I've never had, and probably wouldn't choose to repeat. Twice they take me clubbing and we don't go out until midnight, which is ridiculous, I come home alone at 3am and wake Cassie both times with a drunken message.

On the final night, Dan meets someone he used to go to school with, which Sam and I think is more hilarious the more we drink. We've come all the way to Spain, and he meets a girl, Eva, from around the corner, I leave Sam dancing the night away. My ears are ringing as I walk to the hotel like they used to after Maggie and I had been to see a band, we were frequently deaf the next day, noise pollution was yet to be discovered.

On the journey to the airport, the taxi drives at breakneck speed. We all had too much to drink last night, I should have known better, and we laugh as Sam mimics being sick. I distract myself and acknowledge how proud I am to be able to be their friend and their dad.

I've noticed slight changes in their character and learnt a vast amount about them this week, more than I have in the last couple of years. After what they've been through with their mum, how they think and see the world has changed, I wonder to what extent.

How much of them in front of me is the person they would have become without such a traumatic event?

Dan is forgiving and understanding, he doesn't judge and isn't fazed by any situation, going to university has helped his confidence. He's responsible and I can feel his concern for me with his questions about the changes I'm making in my life. I'm reassuring him I haven't lost my mind, and I do know what I'm doing.

On holiday I watched his chameleon-like personality emerge, he's learnt how to fit in anywhere, people talk to him, and he's developed a laid-back approach attracting attention with his relaxed style in contrast to the quieter gently anxious boy he was, who was happier in the background. If you were in a crisis Dan would be your go-to man.

I can see Sam is coping, he still has some anger but is channelling it positively into making the world a better place. Maisy is his support; she's helped him find a way through his grief and he talks about her non-stop.

He is determined to succeed and excited to discover new things, driven by a clear purpose, I love how passionate he is. As a nurse he'll deal with things I never could, I admire his determination and focus. He has an edge to him and it comes with a bit of attitude. A lot of things are unjust to Sam, he's been shaped and stained by his childhood and will never accept the ordinary. When he was small, he was the loudest in the house and that hasn't changed, we know if he's unhappy.

I had to stop and think while we were away before I shared some of my thoughts with them. What they believe to be true isn't always what I believe, and the way they remember the time around their mum's illness isn't the way I remember it sometimes.

They think differently, and our experiences of that time are unique. I recognise I closed down back then to survive, and I still feel guilty I wasn't present enough for them. We were all reinforcing our boundaries, afraid our lives would give way, not wanting to hurt each other. I couldn't find a way to connect or take on their pain in case it took me underwater and I drowned in it. It's no excuse, Mum says I need to forgive myself and move on, it's easier said than done.

I realise it's a privilege to be in this position, with adult children who choose to spend time with me. They are the people I love the most and I respect them enormously. Some of the mannerisms they display are pure Maggie which makes me smile mostly, but it's tinged with sadness, she will never understand what remarkable human beings we created.

We talked about her in more detail towards the end of the week, digging into some of the awful times we went through but never discussed when we were busy surviving. It felt helpful to talk, we've cried together and this holiday has felt like therapy I didn't know I needed.

As the plane bounces on the tarmac and lands, Dan announces he's arranged to see Eva tonight. Sam and I respond childishly by making loud "oooh" sounds while Dan shakes his head. I'm thinking about Cassie, I'm looking forward to catching up, and telling her about Spain over a relaxed lunch next week.

But tonight I'm going to open the last letter, as soon as I've walked in and unpacked.

2019 – Jody

Ryan and I have been exclusively dating since our third date ten months ago. We meet up almost every other weekend in cheap hotels or an Airbnb because we still live at home, miles away from one another. We're getting very familiar with the bars and cafés in Leicester when we're not in bed, as it's the halfway point and easy to get to from the motorway.

When I'm not with him he texts me constantly, so I know he's definitely interested. He likes me to answer quickly, I try but it's not always possible. He jokes,

"You must be off with someone else."

He takes an interest in what I wear and if my tops are a bit low or my skirts are short, he lets me know kindly, saying,

"I don't want men to get the wrong idea about you."

I don't mind getting changed, attraction-wise I think he's out of my league, and I want to look right for him.

I'm working an early morning shift on reception at the vets when my phone starts to explode with messages bouncing onto my screen. As I glance down, I can see the top one is from Ryan,

"I'm sorry" is all it says.

My phone is on silent, and I'm not supposed to look at it when I'm at the desk, so I try to focus on the neat queue of furry patients in front of me, turning it face down to concentrate on booking them in. The cat with the sore paw is a new patient and she's complaining loudly, the yappy dog isn't helping, he's a regular and here for some injections. A red-eyed owner is last in the queue, she can't speak but I know why she's here, it's the final time we will all see her tortoiseshell tabby today.

When I first started here, I used to cry with the owners when their animals had to be put to sleep, I wasn't much use. One of the nurses said I would never make it, but I showed her I could do it. I'm a professional receptionist here now and a vet's assistant and I love my job. It's not well-paid work, that never mattered to me, I get a kick out of helping, especially animals.

It's nearly lunchtime before I can pick up my phone, more and more patients keep calling and walking in. I try to concentrate on my job and not think about why Ryan is sorry. I take an early lunch and race to the nearest coffee shop around the corner to find out what's going on, the sun is shining through the window onto my screen as I sit and Maisy's message pops up saying,

"I'm sorry, call me" with a sad face, a heart and kisses at the end.

I skim my messages and open Instagram, where four sunny photos appear communicating a clear story I don't want to believe.

In the first one, Ryan's tanned body is draped across a beach-ready blonde who looks like she's been tangoed and needs to eat soon to survive. Her inflatable boobs are on show and she's pouting provocatively with her tongue out for the camera, she looks like a panting dog on heat.

In the second photo, he is lying on top of her, and the electric blue sunbed outlines their squashed bodies, he's got his black swim shorts on, the ones we chose together for this, his first holiday with his friends. I sat patiently as he modelled about ten different styles and colours, strutting up and down the changing room, enjoying more than just my appreciative reaction. His head is turned to the camera and his eyes are glazed, it's how he looks when he's had loads to drink, not dissimilar to his early morning face and the one he has in the middle of sex. I don't look at photos three and four, I don't do anything for a few minutes then I phone Maisy.

2019 – Maisy

When Jody sobs down the phone and begs me to visit her this weekend after Ryan's exploits were exposed online, I can't say no.

She meets me at the station wearing an extra-large floppy hat to hide her face and looks younger without makeup, she looks vulnerable like she's shrunk herself in the wash, her face puffy from wasted tears. I can hear glimpses of the schoolgirl she used to be when she speaks, naïve and impressionable, like the lost girl she once was when she got pregnant with Shaun's baby.

The crying reminds me of when she lost the baby, hours and hours of sitting together on my bed, side by side not speaking much, not knowing what to say but knowing I needed to be there for her. I don't think I feel things as deeply as she does, I don't let many people take root deep inside, she trusts everyone instantly, I give my trust carefully, conscious that people spend a lot of time saying things they don't mean, not on purpose, my childhood taught me that and it's protected me from getting hurt.

When she asked me to go to the riding stables, I thought we were going to look at the horses, stroke them and chat with her friends, how wrong was I?

She finds me a hat in the tack room and a weary-looking pony that doesn't look like it could go very fast. Apparently, it's grey not white, it looks white to me.

She tacks up Sparkle like a professional and I am confident she knows what she's doing when she gently tugs him across the yard to the mounting block so I can get on. She's asked me to ride before and I always say no, she's taking advantage of her situation and we both know it, a wry smile passes between us, an understanding built on years of friendship.

This is my first time on a pony apart from a short ride on a donkey at the seaside when I was about eight, and it looks a long way down. Jody gets on a huge black horse called Rocket; I think that tells us everything we need to know about him.

I start to get nervous thinking I want to get off urgently to go to the bathroom and put my feet on solid ground. Unfortunately, I've seen numerous injuries at the hospital from horse riding and know statistically it's a high-risk activity. One of the downsides of being a nurse is you turn into the health and safety police and start risk-assessing everything.

I remind myself I am doing this for Jody and remember how to breathe again as we set off on a slow walk through the field side-by-side, the expert and the unwilling beginner wobbling about gracelessly.

Jody is the adult in her happy place, turning and leaning down to speak to me, her reins relaxed in one hand, I am sitting as still as I can like a terrified child rigid on their first fairground ride, afraid to move in case something bad happens. After my alcohol shame, I can't go to the hospital again, I need to stay on board. She's talking to me like a competent teacher would, explaining instructions slowly and waiting for me to respond to confirm I've grasped what she's saying. She reassures me patiently,

"You've got a better chance of falling out of bed than falling off Sparkle."

After an hour of wandering in lush green grass and attempting to trot up a muddy little lane with plenty of overhanging branches waiting to kill me, I can't feel my legs.

We retrace our route and head back to the stables, I dismount, I'm pleased with what I've achieved. I've tried something new and quite enjoyed it, not like I want to do it regularly, but it was a challenge, I've succeeded, and Jody has started to talk positively about her future without Ryan so we've both achieved something.

We continue to pick over his annoying habits on the way home like you'd pick through the kitchen bin when you think you've thrown the recycling in there by mistake. The conversation gets worrying as she opens up and describes more about their relationship. Sam and I only saw Ryan's friendly side, polished and perfect, the passive-aggressive behaviour Jody describes, checking her phone, texting constantly on a girl's night out and needing to speak to her immediately for no reason makes me think she's had a lucky escape.

She's hurt and humiliated and having to fight her way through being rejected for the second time, it's hit her hard. Her voice is flat all excitement is drained out, she's tired and needs to retreat from reality for a bit, she's like an injured fox limping towards the forest to rest.

I want to distract her from her life, so I take her for tea at a local pub, and we eat fried food, no salads for us tonight. Jody is drowning her pain in alcohol, and I'm celebrating that she didn't end up with psycho

Ryan. It means our uni food budget will take a battering next month, but several 2-for-1 cocktails and a bottle of wine later we're chatting, laughing, and reminiscing and I know it's worth it.

An idea starts to sprout slowly spreading its shoots, twirling itself around in my brain, rapidly rooting itself like dandelion seeds. I won't mention it to Jody yet, I'll wait until she visits us to put my plan into action. I don't know why I didn't think of him before, I can't wait to speak to Sam.

2019 – Mike

I throw my suitcase on the bed and dig to the bottom to retrieve the letter. I'm not unpacking first. My curiosity is impatient now, I've waited long enough. I agreed with myself to wait until I was home to open it, I didn't want to be distracted from enjoying the present with the boys. Maggie and I would have opened it straight away, I wonder what she would have wanted it to say.

This letter is written on two pages, each side filled with Maggie's mum's neat handwriting. The paper is in reasonable condition, but the horizontal folds across the middle are worn and look like they have been refolded many times, and in places, the ink is wearing off.

I sit propped up on Maggie's side of the bed, leaning against the headboard for support, and read the last letter.

Letter number Eleven

Our Perfect Daughter's Birthday 10th April 1970

Dear John,

My American hero,

When I first found out I was pregnant I never expected to be writing this letter to you, the love of my life. I will never post it, where would I send it now? No one will ever see it, and with that thought comes the freedom to be able to say anything I want, and I want and need to tell you our beautiful daughter has been born. I've called her Maggie. I have put her birthday as the date at the top of the letter, in case you can see it. It felt strange writing it, knowing I would be celebrating this day with her, without you, for the rest of my life.

I was never ashamed of how she was created by us out of pure love. Your love was all-encompassing, taking over every thought, and filling my days with happiness. I never knew I could feel that way, then my letter was returned unopened. I wondered if you had changed your mind about me, I couldn't understand why you hadn't opened my last letter. Mum was trying to convince me you didn't want me, saying how stupid I had been trusting an American. Deep down I think I knew something terrible must have happened to you, I knew you wouldn't leave me like that. It took another week before Laurie's letter arrived, I couldn't believe what was written on the page in front of me, you were dead, died in a plane crash, it was an accident, Mum still wasn't convinced it was true.

I want you to know how happy I was to be pregnant with your child, I was frightened, yes, but it has turned out to be the best thing for me. When I told Mum, she couldn't look at me, she said I had brought shame on the family, her views are so old-fashioned she doesn't understand how the world is changing. Mum wrote me a letter, she said it was easier than trying to talk to me when I wasn't listening, she said I must have the baby adopted. I could go away and have it and no one would know, then I could get on with my life. I would never have done that, I couldn't have given our child away she is the only piece of you I have left, but I didn't know what to do without you, so when Reg asked me to marry him it looked like it was the only way forward.

He came round with the post a few days after I had read Mum's letter, I was sitting on the bottom step in the hall crying, and he could hear me through the glass. He knocked and I let him in and told him everything. I needed someone to talk to, you couldn't tell I was pregnant, my bump was very small, and we got married quickly, Reg insisted, not wanting the stigma of raising a child that wasn't his to fall on him and his family.

I will never love him. I am beginning to care for him, and I am grateful. He's not unkind to me and I will make sure he's kind to Maggie, he's not held her yet. I saw other fathers visiting the hospital, doting on their little girls, connecting with them easily, knowing what to say and I know you would have been like that. How I miss our conversations, the way we could talk openly about love. Reg will provide for us but never love us in the way you would have done, I don't think he knows how. He can't let go, he worries too much about what other people think, he finds it hard to relax, not like you at all.

I would have been with you in America by now, I keep imagining us side by side in rocking chairs on your porch with you holding Maggie, discussing the Beatles splitting up and our future. I keep hearing "Let It Be" on the radio, it has another meaning to me without you here. I would have come there to be with you, I was ready to leave my old life behind. We would have been raising her together, how different my life would be. I am still grieving for you and the life we have lost, I think I will grieve forever, I cry most days. I try not to be sad, and Maggie is the most joyful distraction, I wish you could share my joy. She is exquisite, I keep looking at her closely for signs of you. When I first held her, I wanted to burst with pride, she is beautiful, how clever we were to create her, she is so perfect. When I hold her in my arms I have never felt such a protective love, it flows out of me, and when she squeezes my fingers, I look into her eyes and we smile at each other, we can communicate without speaking it's magical.

I hope you are at peace and can see us from wherever you are. I dream you are looking down on us, keeping us safe, we always say goodnight to you.

I miss you every moment my darling and I will love her, hold her tight and keep her safe for both of us,

Your heartbroken English Rose,

Carole xx

I don't have the right words to describe the joy and sadness conveyed to me in this letter, the contrast is stark. Carole is so grateful for her beautiful baby girl while her heart is breaking with the devastating pain of losing John, her pain is raw, and I hate to think of her feeling this way. I can imagine Carole sitting to write it, as the loving mother she always was, accepting her fate, determined to keep her baby and to hold onto John's love and share Maggie with him somehow. It's as if she's in front of me expressing her thoughts from the two tired pages in my hands, she's finally telling her story.

I phone Cassie and read her the letter; I can hear the emotion catch in her voice when she suggests coming over to do some detective work to try and help me trace John's sister, Laurie. It is the logical next step, and one I need to take with her encouragement and several glasses of wine and a curry.

Part 3

"Being Brave"
2020, 2021

2020 – Sam

I knew James liked Jody from the second she walked into the pub. Since living with him in his bungalow I can read his expressions before he speaks, it's like living with another version of Dan. He didn't need to say anything, his raised eyebrow spoke volumes for him.

Maisy rushed up to hug Jody and I followed. When Jody saw James she automatically hugged him too. He held on to her for a fraction too long making Jody blush and giggle like the girl I remember from a few years ago.

We are executing Maisy's plan, she's engineered this meeting, it's taken her months, thankfully early indications are promising. James didn't take much persuading, but Jody needed Maisy's careful manipulation to be here. After Ryan, she's adamant she doesn't want to think about dating, but she is willing to meet James on a strictly platonic basis if that's understood.

Within minutes James and Jody are sitting leg to leg, smiling and joking, if you didn't know them, you'd think they were a couple, mirroring gestures and taking a drink at the same time, they're oblivious to everyone else. Maisy and I exchange amused glances as they chat animatedly leaving no room for us to speak, I lean in and listen.

They are presenting potted histories of their lives, the fillet steak versions, treading cautiously and hunting for common ground, like learning a new dance step, putting your best foot forward while trying to protect your toes. I hope I never have to go through this stage again, I don't see myself with anyone but Maisy.

James heads to the toilet and I follow.

Mate "I've just met my future," is his only comment. I haven't met this James before, but I know he's deadly serious because he doesn't mess people about.

The attraction is mutual, Maisy and I might as well not be there. He puts his hand on her leg, it's a sign of affection and ownership and she looks at him quizzically, the sexual tension fizzes between them and playful gestures land on arms and legs, each one braver and more intimate than the last, challenging and cooperating in their private mating language. Maisy whispers that they're like monkeys grooming and picking insects off each other or horses biting and nipping, connecting with affection.

When they remember we are there we decide to move on to a club. They walk hand in hand and Jody looks back at us and sticks her tongue out in a "so what" gesture. Once inside they dance, circling with primeval behaviour, before he pulls her closer and holds her tightly, his arms attached firmly to her waist. He's looking down at her and she's reflecting his loving face, like a flower opening for the sun, how poetic, it must be the alcohol. We get glimpses of her laughing as the club lighting shoots past, Maisy and I are happily redundant, and we turn away.

We leave the club before they do and return home. In the taxi Maisy talks about Jody's past relationships and I wonder why James broke off his engagement before he came to uni, and why I haven't asked him about it. I think they've both been damaged by past relationships. We contemplate how lucky we are to have one another, and I get a glimpse of future Maisy when she is the anxious parent, wondering what time her child will come home tonight.

We make love in the way you can when no one else is home. Maisy can still surprise me, we know every inch of each other's bodies, she is beautiful, and I'm turned on before she takes off her clothes. We are noisy, carefree and adventurous, being slightly drunk helps us to experiment and ask for whatever we want. She wants me to be dominant and take control, so I become a doctor and examine her thoroughly, face first.

She is sleeping in my arms when the front door slams and two voices enter the house, each unsuccessfully telling the other to be quiet. James' bedroom door opens, and the house falls silent for a few short hours, not long enough for a good night's sleep.

I wake to the sound of crashing pans, and the smell of bacon forces me out of bed and into the kitchen to investigate, Maisy doesn't move.

Jody is sitting at the kitchen table in James' Arctic Monkeys T-shirt and he's animatedly chatting as he cooks breakfast. It's like a scene from a cooking show with Jody as the famous guest waiting to share her limited opinions on the quality of the food. Maisy walks in and squeals when she sees Jody, they hug like long-lost friends. I know Maisy can't wait to be alone with her to find out what happened last night.

James puts the food down, with kitchen roll for napkins, and sits next to Jody opposite us. They are glued together on the narrow bench with secret smiles in their private club of two. Breakfast finished and there's no signs of them moving. They're making plans for their day together, as if this is what they do every weekend. We leave them to it and get back into bed, but not before Maisy's bounced on it with excitement, she can't control her arms and legs and does star jumps haphazardly in the air.

The following weekend we meet up as a foursome, this time we go out for a meal. They are serious and they've updated Maisy separately about just how serious they are. Jody in long conversations and messages every night saying she can't believe how perfect he is, and James by floating through the house whistling and singing cheesy songs incessantly and thanking her in a jokey way for having the best friend in the universe.

James and Jody have spoken every day and already talked about visiting James' parents. They've deleted their dating apps, so they are officially exclusive. I think it's happened very fast, but Maisy is delighted with her work and is wondering who she can play Cupid for next.

2020 - Mike

Moving day has finally arrived after the solicitor has caused chaos, it's a sunny day with no clouds, it feels like a good omen. Dan and I have spent the last few months forensically dissecting each room, manically cleaning, and pulling apart our family lives which existed within their walls. Re-living the painful memories in the process, ripping them from us like removing a plaster too quickly, tearing at the skin.

At least I've sold it to a family I like, they have two young children who are younger than ours were when we moved in. An awful man came to view after the family left, he pointed out how much work needed doing and said it wasn't worth the money. I was going to ask the estate agent to take over the viewings after him, how can you be impartial about selling your family home? I couldn't unplug my emotions, fortunately the family offered the asking price, I couldn't have sold it to the rude, critical man, Maggie wouldn't have wanted him to have it.

It's been mentally and physically exhausting preparing to leave and it's involved many beers and takeaways to get us through, my waistline is complaining. It is difficult not to turn the fun and laughter we had as a family here into sadness, a sense of loss follows us like a bad smell no air freshener can mask.

I am trying to hang onto some of the joy and be grateful for the happy times we had when the boys were younger growing up here, but it's hard. I break down when I sit on a pile of boxes where our bed was, you can see the square indentations in the cream carpet from where the legs used to be.

Maggie loved our bedroom, it was her retreat, our escape from the outside world, a calm contemplative passionate space, although in the early years the children bounded in every morning, bringing their energy and optimism with them.

When the afternoon sun was streaming in it was her favourite reading spot. I'd find her propped up on top of the covers book in hand, admiring a view of the changing seasons from the trees across the road. I'd always bring her a cup of tea, we didn't need anything fancy in our lives to be content, we were enough, that's how you know you've found the right person.

Moments play out in my head, snapshots of time saved in my memory bank, racing forward, stalling, rewinding and pausing at powerful points. It's amazing the detail that surfaces from years ago, all the sounds, smells and colours stored, patiently waiting for me to stop and find them. I try to remember the minor details, stepping in to absorb the sensations before my memories fade and dissolve, like melting snow when a fresh fall piles on top, a showreel of the supreme bits, the highlights, each jostling for centre stage.

In the hallway of my new apartment, I tentatively hammer a nail into the freshly painted wall, and hang one of the last photographs of Maggie, me and the boys. I place it next to one of Maggie on our wedding day, her beautiful eyes are shining back at me full of hope, holding my gaze, where did the years go?

The photograph of John from Carole's precious box is in a silver frame on the kitchen windowsill, he deserves to be visible for everyone to see, I want him in the room we're likely to spend the most time in. I intend to tell his and Carole's story, it feels important I do that for Maggie. All the letters are together at last, numbers ten and eleven reunited with the others in their original box, I've moved them to a dining room cupboard so we can re-read them and re-live our family history whenever we want and be proud of their love and the daughter they created.

I've reflected over the past weeks about the randomness of recent events. If I hadn't decided to move house, we wouldn't know John and Laurie existed, and if I had packed up the loft instead of Dan I wonder if I'd have opened those boxes, probably not. Questions with no answers make me think about how many secrets are sitting in lofts and cellars, and how many children don't know their parents are not their birth parents for all sorts of reasons. I contemplate for whose benefit these secrets are kept before Cassie interrupts my thinking. She's come to help me unpack with a roller and paint tray balanced on one hand, a plastic takeaway bag gripped in the other and a bottle of red wine tucked under her arm.

2020 – Jody

I am trying and failing not to overthink what to wear to meet James' parents. I want to make the right impression, I need to look like the girl that is right for their son, his perfect girlfriend.

I send Maisy four photos of me in different outfits. First is a conservative green dress to the knee with three-quarter sleeves, she says I look like a politician's wife with no personality. Outfit number two is a flowery jumpsuit with no sleeves, I think it makes me look a bit short, and like I'm missing a pair of roller skates and a tray of food. The third option is an outfit I wore for a wedding, a formal navy silk suit, it instantly turns me into an older person, I look like I am trying too hard.

Maisy and I agree on outfit number four, smart jeans a respectable red top with white hearts on, short black wedge boots and not much cleavage or make-up, it says girl next door but with her own opinion. I pace up and down in it, practising my entrance. James has been planning to take me home to meet his parents for ages, but his mum has been working away and I cover some weekends at the vets so this is the first weekend that works for everyone.

Since Maisy and Sam introduced us, we haven't stopped talking and laughing, it's effortless being with him, he's the easiest person to get on with. We were relaxed like old friends from the beginning, it's completely different from my other relationships. I don't have to change who I am, because he loves me for me, I'm not second-guessing what to say or preparing subjects to talk about in advance. I couldn't believe it when he said he loved me after two weeks.

I can tell him anything. All the craziness goes around in my head and when I'm anxious, he calmly works through it with me and tells me how special I am, how unique. He's the first person I've ever met who doesn't want to change me in some way, we fit together perfectly. He's more intelligent than me and will explain things patiently when I don't get it, without getting cross or making me feel stupid. We don't agree on everything, and I like being able to voice my opinion and then sit and watch as James weighs it up, turning it over in his mind. He debates with himself, moving his lips and hands, patting one hand on top of the other as he thinks, it reminds me of firming down sand on top of a sandcastle.

We leave James' house late morning to arrive in Durham in time for lunch. I've asked James every question I can think of on the journey to get an idea about what his mum and dad might be like. He keeps reassuring me, "They will love you." I want to believe him.

I've got plenty of time to catastrophise, the traffic is terrible. I've always enjoyed being trapped in a car with people I love. Dad and I used to talk in the car on the way to swimming practice or school, it was our catch-up time. We had more dad-and-daughter conversations in our car where he couldn't be distracted, than anywhere else.

Before me, James has only brought two girls home. The last one was the daughter of a family friend, they were engaged, but it ended badly. He found out she was seeing his best friend, so he lost her, and his best friend, which I think he regrets from the way he spoke about him. I was silent and listened when he re-lived the pain from two years ago, honoured that he trusted me to share the hurt. I felt secure enough to try to explain how getting pregnant when I was still at school was arguably the worst thing and the best thing to have happened to me. We both looked down when we started speaking, sad and reflective sharing powerful intimate stories that jolted us forward to grow up quickly, events that influenced how we live our lives now. We stopped at the services and James gently pushed my chin up so I faced him, staring into his eyes. He said I had nothing to be ashamed of and held me as I cried for the little girl who'd unnecessarily carried the shame, like extra baggage, along with her to this point, I completely ruined my make-up.

We drive down the huge driveway to his family home, it reminds me of a mansion on a film set. We've chatted for the whole journey, now my mouth is dry and I can't think of anything to say. I am desperate to make a suitable impression, to not say or do anything awkward, I'm not great when I'm nervous and meet new people.

His parents come out of their home and down some marble steps to greet us like actors in a play, greeting their arriving guests in an Agatha Christie murder mystery. They are closely followed by a cute black labrador who makes a beeline for James, they've missed each other.

James introduces me,

"Murphy meet Jody." Murphy sniffs me suspiciously, checking me out before jumping up and licking my face, I love how accepting dogs are.

His mum gives me a big hug and says he's told her so much about me she feels she knows me already. His dad hugs me too, he has the same amused look James has most of the time, as if comedians are playing on a loop in his head, mouth twitching, eyes crinkling, I have watched his face for hours.

When James introduces me, he makes me feel important and valued, like I have been elevated from someone's reserve choice of basic beans on cheap white toast to their ideal breakfast. I am now a portion of granary sourdough dressed in butter and topped with avocado, rocket and two skilfully poached eggs, with sriracha artfully drizzled on top and a sprinkle of chilli flakes to make me perfect. I am distracting my mind, and I need to concentrate.

We are having a barbecue in the staggeringly beautiful garden. The food is similar to the type of thing my mum would prepare at home. When Maisy used to come, she'd say it was posh people's food, she always ate loads. At her house it was burgers and sausages, here it's kebabs, marinated chicken, deli-style salads and Waitrose delicious puddings. It's very relaxed and informal and they try hard to involve me in conversation. We drink elderflower gin; I feel sophisticated and privileged to be here. They downplay the house and his mum's successful career, she waves her hands as she says,

"Right place, right time, I've been lucky." I think she's hugely talented.

The next morning as we tucked into smoked salmon and perfectly scrambled eggs, his dad innocently asked if I slept ok. We stayed in James' old room, and I fought off his numerous attempts to interest me in sex, so we exchanged glances before I answered honestly, "Yes, thank you."

Last night I was adamant nothing would happen and repeated,

"It would be disrespectful when it's my first night here, I'll worry about every noise we make," like some Victorian lady. He laughed and said that's why he loves me so much.

Now I'm super pleased nothing happened.

We leave after breakfast with a dozen fresh eggs from their hens, some of the eggshells are a beautiful shade of powder blue. It reminds me of my mum years ago, baking extra and giving it to Maisy to take home. I miss Mum for a fleeting moment before James puts "I Bet You Look Good on the Dancefloor" on in the car and I re-live the night we met for the thousandth time, it's our song, the first one we danced to the night he changed my life.

After last night it feels like our connection has grown and deeper feelings have landed. He's so happy I like his parents and says his mum whispered, "she's lovely," before we left. It's weird because butterflies cause chaos when I think about us, having a party inside me before I see him, but as soon as he holds me or touches my hand, I am calm.

We are turning into James' street when my phone rings, it's Mum. Dad is in hospital he's had a heart attack.

James doesn't ask me anything or need to think about what he should do; he turns the car around and puts the name of the hospital into his sat nav. As we head from Newcastle to Derbyshire down the motorway, I know he's my person, the one I want to be with forever.

I imagine every terrible outcome as the drive takes longer than ever before, James keeps looking at me saying it will be ok. Images I'd forgotten flash up from memorable times with Dad. Pushing me on the swing at the park, encouraging me to go higher, blindly trusting him and nervously holding on. Dad patiently teaching me to ride my pink unicorn bike one snowy Christmas, when I insisted on going outside to practice even though what I was asking was impossible with the deep snow. More recently, Dad taking my hand in the car on the way to my first day at secondary school, with neither of us needing to say anything.

When we arrive, Dad is sitting up in bed, he's pale and has a tube in his arm, otherwise, he's fine. He makes light of his situation saying it's not the way he was planning to meet James. I don't tell him off for scaring me to death, but I want to. Dad and James exchange a look and their love for me passes between them, I swallow hard to stop myself from crying.

Mum and Dad think it would be helpful to fill him in on the quirky things I did and said as a child, so he knows what he's getting himself into. I sigh and object to the psychiatric analysis, playfully blaming their questionable parenting for my flaws. We have the most natural conversation in an unnatural environment with everyone trading stories at my expense. I look around the room at the faces I love most and consciously bank this powerful memory, I'm beyond grateful they are all still safe.

After a couple of hours together, James takes me home to Mum and Dad's, they should be coming back tomorrow, he wouldn't think of leaving me alone tonight. They're keeping Dad in for observation, but it's nothing to worry about.

Walking through my front door with James by my side completes our backstories. We understand each other, our family values are similar, and it's easy to understand the people we've become when you look at where we came from. Poppy joins us on the bed that night and I listen to her purr rattle as James falls asleep. I keep stroking her, comforting us both, unable to sleep, thinking about what the other outcomes could have been and how fragile life is.

When Dad comes home the following morning, he asks me to follow him into the garden, and I follow him into his shed, it's a man cave really, with a kitchen area where he makes us tea.

We sit, and he looks at me with tears in his eyes taking his time to speak,

"I am sorry." He pauses, composing himself.

"Sorry for the way I treated you and froze you out when I found out you were pregnant. I didn't know how to handle it. I've tried to rationalise it, and I think in my mind you went to bed as my little girl and when I woke up, you were a fully grown pregnant young lady.

Naively, I hadn't realised I needed to navigate the water in between, that it was my job to build a bridge and fill the gap. I couldn't recognise my little girl, and I couldn't understand that you were still in there somewhere, and I didn't know you might still need me, selfishly I felt redundant, despite what your mum tried to tell me. I'm not excusing how I behaved, it was wrong, I need to try to explain because I love you so much and I want you to know it was my fault I wasn't supportive, not yours. I hope you can forgive me."

He looks directly at me when he speaks and I see the businessman in my dad taking accountability for his actions, wanting desperately to make things right. It's not a well-rehearsed speech and I can see how much hurt has been simmering beneath his words, he's been forcing the lid back onto a pan of boiling water. I don't know what to say, I let him off the hook and hug him tightly and manage,

"It's okay Dad."

We walk inside arm in arm hoping for a slice of Mum's famous family cake to find a fruit platter offered on the breakfast bar. Dad's healthy heart diet has begun. Dad and I know Mum never does things by halves, so we'll be embracing her healthy living plan from now on whether we like it or not.

James leaves after lunch, I don't want him to go, he promises to come at the weekend and I physically ache when he drives away.

The three of us sit exhausted in the kitchen, Dad openly brings up more awkward subjects I didn't know we'd been avoiding. The conversations are measured discussions, we all get to have our opinions, and on some things, we don't align. It's like Mum and Dad need to say everything tonight in case the world ends tomorrow. Dad's heart attack has changed our relationship, he's allowing me to tread over an invisible line into the adult-daughter space, I am proceeding with caution like a newborn giraffe finding its legs, unsure of what's expected.

As we get ready for bed, they say they love James and Mum ends the evening by future scaping about what she will wear for our wedding. Dad and I laugh at her, but truthfully, I've wondered what sort of dress I will wear too.

2020 – Mike

Laurie Gray is a stunning-looking lady. As Dan and I walk to the far corner of the coffee shop to meet Maggie's Aunt, I feel like we are on Long-Lost Families, where the cameras capture every emotion, hoping for plenty of tears. I feel raw and exposed, I'm battling to reign in the emotion.

I've given her a brief outline of events leading up to today, from the letters Maggie's mum and Laurie's brother exchanged. She didn't know her niece existed before we got in touch. It must be unsettling, to find a part of your brother is still walking this earth. Then after a lifetime of not knowing each other, discovering the reality of Maggie's illness means she will never understand who you are, it's a lot to take in.

I'm startled by how much she looks like Maggie, with the same petite frame, green eyes, and a welcoming smile. Laurie is the image of how Maggie will look in the future, we hug tightly. She's struggling to control her feelings, apologising and dabbing at her face with a handkerchief while scrutinising Dan.

When Cassie and I found Laurie on Facebook, the family resemblance was clear, but in the flesh, I'm unsettled by the similarity, it's a relief when she speaks, and her American accent brings me back to the present. She thinks Dan looks a lot like her son did when he was younger, Dan is visibly pleased with the connection saying he would love to meet him one day.

We chat non-stop filling in the gaps from over fifty years of our family history, trying to imprint on one another the connected DNA that has been missing for so long. It's like a marathon of memories running towards the finish line, stopping at each mile to give new information about key events in our lives.

Coffee turns into lunch, and we drop Laurie at her hotel late afternoon. I promise to pick her up the next morning to visit Maggie at Greenacres. I pray Maggie will be having a reasonable day tomorrow, I want Laurie to like her. Afterwards, we plan to go to her uncle's grave, visiting their uncle was why John came to

England when he met Carole all those years ago, we are completing the circle.

The next day I am nervous when we walk into Greenacres and still praying that Maggie is having a good day. I know it's Friday from the comforting smell of fried fish resting in the air. It follows us along the corridor as we head towards the day room, for some reason I apologise for it, even though it's nothing to do with me. Laurie has enough grace to easily laugh off my discomfort and reassure me it's fine.

Maggie is sitting in a low chair calmly studying the garden. I introduce Laurie as an old friend when we sit down. Laurie talks about plants and Maggie nods as if she understands every word, listening to her enthuse about nature's perfect palette. Watching them they could easily be mistaken for mother and daughter sitting and chatting amiably as if this occurs every day. Maggie keeps looking at her, I want to believe she knows Laurie is special and important in her life, maybe a part of her recognises something familiar, maybe I want this to be the case and maybe if I want it enough, I can convince myself it's true.

The spell is broken when Maggie gets up to go to her room, she doesn't say anything just removes herself from us, leaving her slippers behind. Laurie's composure crumbles as she watches Maggie's back disappear. I hold her tight, wishing it wasn't this way, knowing she would have made the most fantastic aunt.

It begins to drizzle as we leave Maggie, and a cold wind is whistling through the graveyard when we get out of the car. It's like winter has decided to arrive early, I mention this to Laurie, and she jokes about the British obsession with the weather, breaking up our solemn walk. I never know how to behave in a cemetery, other cultures treat death in different ways, I want to be respectful obviously, but I hope when I die people are thinking and talking about happier times.

Serious lines of grass and stone form regimented rows, however, the visit to the graveside is unexpectedly amusing and provides light relief from my scrambling brain. Their uncle had a wicked sense of humour and chose to have "Hi! Thanks for stopping by!" inscribed at the bottom of his headstone which Laurie kept a secret until we were standing there.

We didn't take flowers, Laurie loves flowers, "But not when they die on top of the grave appreciated by no one, certainly not the sleeping dead," she said.

Instead, we called in at Greenacres on the way home and dropped off three impressive bunches each with twelve red roses, to remember Carole, and for everyone to enjoy.

When Laurie comes for tea to meet Sam, Maisy, and Cassie, she feels like part of our family. After spending two days together we are joking comfortably, celebrating our families' real personalities and sharing stories like you do with friends you've known for ages. She is a contradiction, delicate and robust, quiet and loud, she's all the instruments in an orchestra with a wealth of extreme expressions for every conversation.

We learn about John as a brave young man in the Air Force, fighting for his country, before he met Carole. She reminisces for us, sharing highlights from their childhood bringing it vividly to life. Laurie explains why she would never move house,

"I don't want to move the memories; I like them right where they are."

She's emotional and exposed when she says, "I didn't know if I could survive without him."

I feel protective, Maggie would love her, she's witty and strong and some of her mannerisms are pure Maggie.

When the boys and I drive Laurie to the airport she asks us to visit her soon. We promise we won't pass up the opportunity to stay in America with free accommodation, she laughs and tells us the more of us that visit the better, she's not going anywhere. As I hug her for the final time, I feel connected to her in the way a tree is connected to the earth, grounded, and vital for survival. Her impact is powerful, and I am ready to grow and move forward in my life partly because of her.

My job has always been just a job, full of rules and restrictions, I have been defined by process and procedure, and it suited me to be in constant control. Now I want to change my job and make a difference, If I don't do it soon, then when? I've seen the impact that getting to know us is having on Laurie and I don't underestimate the joy we are bringing to each other's lives. Recent events have sparked something in me and the idea of working in research, to help people trace their birth families, keeps crossing my mind. I have time to learn and retrain, I don't need to earn a big salary to support the boys, they are nearly grown up. I want to do something valuable, something with meaning.

It's exciting stepping out of the old Mike, the fit doesn't feel right yet, and the new model requires work, I need to develop my confidence. The way I look on the outside, the calm and controlled me is helpfully betraying what is happening on the inside. Trepidation and fear regularly spiral into panic as everything I face is new and the outcomes are unknown, but my self-belief is growing. I have pushed myself, felt the fear and done it anyway, and the more I push the more I like it.

After what happened to Maggie I am finally emerging from my old life and living again, I know she would be proud and supportive cheering me on. I can hear her in my head sometimes as if she's standing next to me, speaking to me as she spoke to the boys, "Go on you can do it, you can do anything, be anything, I love you."

It's the same chant she used with them when they were learning to walk and swim, or before their exams, she used it anytime they needed encouragement. Sam would roll his eyes with a "Mum is off again," glance across at me or Dan, it's the insignificant things I remember the most. Her bespoke phrases, her gestures, the way she fiddled with her rings when she was nervous, the intimate things a lover notices. I'm regularly disarmed by a smell that take me back to the past. I walked behind a lady in town last week and she smelt like Maggie, she was wearing her perfume and looked similar, I had to stop walking and sit on a bench, I needed a second to breathe, it's those things that catch me out. I don't think Maggie wears any perfume now.

We had a secret language like all established couples, we used it to go home early from boring dinner parties or to leave a tedious work do, one of us making excuses to help the other. Giggling, racing to the car like naughty school children pretending they are ill to get out of class, I miss her laugh.

I can think about Maggie and Cassie in the same sentence so that's progress, it's only been doable since I moved house, maybe I had to physically move away from our joint life to be able to gravitate forward.

Grief dances to its own tune and no matter how many times I try to stop the music it starts up again, like a cut you keep catching, leaking blood before the next scab appears. They won't go away, the thoughts, the memories, the feelings I had when she was diagnosed, and I wouldn't want them to. I will never get over losing my Maggie to Alzheimer's, but I'm learning to live with the emotions it's created. I'm carrying them with me in a box in my mind, I keep a tight lid on it, only occasionally does the jack-in-a-box pop up and surprise me.

2020 – Shaun

It's now or never.

I walk past the predictable chain stores and restaurants across Oxford's town centre as I focus on my mission.

I reach the less salubrious parts, the bits you discover as a student who lives here, the not-for-tourist streets, and need a drink. I stop at a small grubby pub for a pint, it's the size of a large living room, and ask my logical brain if I can do this. I convincingly argue for and against myself like I'm accusing and defending the same witness. As the pint goes down, I get to my feet, decisively signalling the silent cross-examination is over. The legal team "for" have won. I am on my way to an "open mic" night to do my first stand-up.

My regular footsteps provide the ideal rhythm for my final rehearsal, slowly pacing out the lines. I know the material well; I've memorised it to exam standards and I'm exceptional at exams. I've been writing anecdotes from my life for a while and questioning why I want to be a lawyer. Ady did me a favour introducing me to a whirlwind of drama I knew nothing about on-stage and off it, providing stacks of material for me to write.

I enter an anti-climax. Eight people are standing propping up the bar, it's lighter inside than I remember, I think I'm too early. I stride purposefully past the bar to the sign-up table; I've watched other people do this on previous visits when I came to check it out and tried to guess what their acts might be. I write my name in capital letters on the sheet, after I make sure I don't know anyone in the room, I don't, that's a relief. The wait begins.

I sit near the front at a table for two, taking in the makeshift wooden decking in front of me masquerading as a stage. The carpet once maroon has seen better days, and posters advertising student nights, 2-for-1 beer and a band playing this weekend are plastered everywhere in place of wallpaper or paint.

An older, longhaired heavily tanned man, who looks like he'd be more comfortable surfing than in this dingy bar, sets up the microphone. He walks off the stage and the nerves kick in; I wonder what I think I'm doing as the lights go down.

I stare at one lonely metal stand on an empty stage and try to manifest success, ready for when I'm standing there, preparing myself as athletes do, running the race on repeat in their heads where they win every time.

I've no idea what the two acts up there before me said. The first one, a drag artist reminded me of Ady, the way he stood was familiar with confidence and arrogance spewing out. When my name is called, I have an out-of-body experience, I don't remember getting on stage. I haven't told them it's my first time I don't want their sympathy.

I grip tightly onto a piece of card that I cut from the cereal box this morning, with bullet points written on it to remember the order of everything in case my brain stalls, it's unlikely but not impossible. I try to cover the back when I realise you'll see a bowl of Cocoa Pops if I hold it up. I look uncomfortably towards the bar as I reach the mic, I can't make eye contact I need to talk to the far wall. Then I have a crisis of confidence and look down when I launch into my first anecdote, "The Early Years."

I'm using self-deprecating humour about a shy gay boy's life, living in semi-rural Oxford, telling risky stories concerning the amount of time he spent locked in his bedroom. I move on to material relating to my time at school, using acerbic witty observations involving my parents, and how I reluctantly conformed to parental expectation and followed the traditional route to university, finishing this part of my set with,

"And here I am Mum and Dad, how proud are you now? This wasn't in your birth-to-death life plan was it!"

I hear a random laugh, I think it might be landing ok, no one is heckling. I keep going, delivering my material like a monologue, hands by my side, frozen to the spot, my body is motionless like the proverbial rabbit caught in the headlights, I forget to pause and am hardly looking up.

When I get to the final part of my act, the car crash story, I acknowledge where I am, and begin to settle in. I glance at the bar and the numbers have doubled; everyone is looking at me. I consciously gesture to illustrate the best bits and start to play to the crowd, exaggerating wildly as the laughter increases. The applause makes me perform a low bow, I can't remember ever bowing before.

Who am I when I'm up here?

I walk towards the bar to collect my free pint for performing and someone shouts, "Well done mate," I raise my hand as if I do this every day and as the adrenaline pumps around, I wonder if my law career might be over before it's started.

I find another club the following week to go through the whole experience again. I stop for a pint on the way, knowing I'm getting on stage this time, superstitious that if I don't go for a pint first it will go wrong, while internally arguing logically, that this is a ridiculous way to think.

Scanning the room I count 51 heads in the audience, I'm on second to last. They've had plenty to drink this time, I've practised moving my body and arms, it should help to keep me present and make me look up and out into the darkness. I want to appear less like a remote-controlled robot and more relaxed and relatable.

My final applause is accompanied by cheers of "more" and stamping feet. At the end, again, I bow dramatically, it's a part of my act now and I'm ironically humble and grateful. Inside I'm flying out of control, their approval is addictive.

I spend the following few months doing one or two open mic nights a week in local pubs, testing and finessing my material, trying new stuff to see what gets the biggest reaction. It doesn't get easier, the nerves are painful pre-gig, it's a familiar sensation now. After the first two sentences are delivered, I relax and I start living for the silent drumbeat at the end, before the applause, it's the moment I'm proud of myself for getting up there.

When I walk into a pub on a rainy Tuesday night and see Sam and Maisy I panic, and join them at the bar, deciding with each sip if I can go through with it if they're in the audience. I don't care what strangers think or that's what I'm telling myself, but what they think counts and if it doesn't go well, we'll talk about it for years. I've enjoyed keeping this from my friends and family, stepping outside what's expected from me without any judgement.

I neck a couple of shots and tell Sam I'm going the toilet, then head to the stage, I'm on last. Sam and

Maisy look confused when they see me up there, like seeing your parents in a new way when you find out they still have sex. I'm another Shaun when I'm on stage.

They are the loudest in the crowd and make the people chatting around them stop and listen. Maisy gives me a thumbs up early on as I freestyle and mention that my mates are in, and they've been together since school. It's greeted with "aarghs" and applause when I play on their devotion to nursing, comparing their vocation to my shallow existence as a lawyer in waiting -

"Waiting for the big pay cheques to roll in."

I am dripping with sweat when I join them at the bar. Sam keeps staring at me and shaking his head.

I say "What?" and he doesn't speak.

Maisy is jumping on the spot saying "You were brilliant. How? When?" Sam is still shaking his head.

We go for a pizza, and I apologise as the rush of adrenaline drips out of my body onto the table. I say out loud for the first time what I've been thinking for months, I want to leave my law degree to become a comedian.

I watch Sam and Maisy take in the news. Maisy laughs, her wide eyes tell me what she thinks until she realises I'm serious, then she switches to being supportive, she's a "follow your dreams" type of girl. Sam knows my parents won't accept the news so for the remainder of dinner, I use Maisy and Sam as a test case. They become my parents, and I work on convincing them before I work out how to convince my actual parents it's a decent idea.

A few days later, I venture home to Mums, ready for a challenging conversation about my future. I've been rehearsing my arguments obsessively, reassuring and reminding myself it is my life, and I get to choose which direction it goes in.

Mum is pleased to see me and furious within five minutes, she's not equipped with the empathy required to understand another perspective. I'm Shaun, straight A's, off to Oxford, first-class law degree, become a lawyer, meet a nice girl, buy a house in an acceptable postcode with a garden, get married and have a family, this was Mum and Dad's unspoken plan when I was born.

It's not gone her way, first Dad left, so she had to parent alone and quit the career she loved, to be there for me, then she had to work through my sexuality and reset her expectations. Not that I won't get married one day and have a family, but it will be different from the one she'd neatly arranged in her head.

My news about leaving university renders her silent, except for her index finger, tapping on the kitchen counter as she tries to process what I'm saying. Smoke would be pluming out of her ears if she was a cartoon character, but she's smart, she doesn't raise her voice, she asks me to sit down, "I'm prepared to talk about all the options."

I'm under no illusion how panicked she is when she facetimes Dad for extra ammunition. She puts him on speakerphone and places him in the centre of the table, propped up by the fruit bowl, his face is surprised by the call.

Mum and Dad are a united front, which is rare, and Dad is a top-class lawyer. He is very vocal with their opinion and talks about wasting opportunities. After they have finished dominating the space and dictating what I will do, I end up agreeing not to do anything drastic. We agree that I will get to the end of the third year before I make any firm decisions. I walk out of Mum's front door with an uncomfortable sense of having let myself down.

So, I carry on as promised and work towards my law degree, with their words of "how proud they are," and "following in the family footsteps," ringing in my ears, but the weight of their expectation makes me resent them and I ignore their calls. They have won education-wise, the trade-off is we have no relationship.

I perform comedy occasionally and wonder if my parents probably do know best.

Is it really a career I can succeed in? The odds are stacked against me. Why would I want to risk everything?

I let the old version of Shaun resettle around me, he's familiar and not remotely challenging. I grudgingly accept that I might have to be here studying for another few years to become a lawyer after I complete my first degree, it's beginning to feel inevitable until Ady reappears.

2021 - Mike

It started as a harmless game with silly flirting at the bar, honestly, I was relieved to have somebody to talk to. After my "Eureka" moment career-wise, I'd booked a training course to learn more about what a job researching family history would entail, I wanted to be sure it was the right choice for me. I hoped to understand the skills needed, see if I was a good fit, and address any gaps in my knowledge.

Two nights away just outside Manchester, marooned intentionally at a hotel that had been dropped onto a golf course in the middle of nowhere. It was nice, with a lake to walk around, the grounds needed some attention, and the photos online had promised greater things, but it was fine.

I was nervous driving up the motorway and waiting in reception for the trainer to collect the five of us, I felt like the new boy at school. When you lose someone from your everyday life you have to get used to doing things on your own, not that Maggie would have been here with me, but she would have helped with the planning and packing and called me in the car, checking up on me, knowing I would find this situation quite stressful.

I noticed her when I was checking in and walked across the echoey marble floor to join her, trying to walk softly so I didn't make much noise. We brushed legs as I sunk further than expected into the plush red velvet sofa and landed heavily beside her, she glanced up from her phone and smiled. She was expensively dressed and appeared a similar age, possibly a few years younger.

We didn't speak until the break when we queued for coffee, she commented on the biscuits being animal-shaped, and I laughed and joked,

"It reminds me of my mum's baking and icing elephant biscuits with her when I was a child, shaking too many hard silver balls on the top and my dad complaining they would break his teeth."

It was meant to be an icebreaker, a talking point, and we obligingly broke the ice over the biscuits when this stranger smiled and connected with me.

When the five of us came down for dinner on the first night, we met in the bar. She made a beeline for me, I was pleased as the other three were a lot chattier and discussing football, it was enjoyable to have some feminine company and flattering. I kept wondering if she was my type. It's not easy to know what your type is when you've lived with one woman your whole adult life. I liked her. The way she carried herself, she had a positive presence, bubbly, funny and tiny, not even five foot tall. She made it clear she was single, and when she spoke her voice was deep and strong, it sounded like it belonged to a much bigger person. She was confident and that was attractive, I couldn't stop thinking about her as I was lying in bed that night, trying to decide how much I liked her and if I should ask her out for a drink.

She joined me at breakfast, she didn't ask if she could join me, she sat down opposite as if we'd previously arranged it. Smelling like oranges and lemons, looking like she should have been working on a cosmetics counter in a department store, spraying perfume and irritating people, but with her winning smile she'd make you forgive her. I was equally interested, awkward and terrified.

Over breakfast, I noticed how she cut her food into even pieces, each move consciously considered, carefully sizing up which piece of toast and egg to eat next, planning with precision, creating an orderly procession of perfect yellow and white squares like an abstract work of art with lines of added ketchup. I should have known then she was a lady who always had a plan.

She drank her coffee black, and I silently worried for the stains on her teeth, before checking in with myself and thinking I should get out more.

The course was interesting and by day two we were relaxing and participating, happily sharing a chapter or two from the edited stories of our lives. I wanted to do well in front of her, for her to think highly of me, I'm not sure why I cared. I needed to be the star pupil and hear her praise me in her loud gravelly voice which got deeper when she laughed.

I didn't think before I went to her room on the second night, the volume of wine at dinner pushed me forward.

We kissed in the lift on the way up and I felt as if it was happening to another me, like I was an actor playing a part, I've seen an abundance of films with this scene in. I had forgotten I could feel this way driven by pure lust, I was wanted and desired again. I felt free in that moving metal box.

When the doors opened, she took my hand, and I followed her inside her room. I looked at the bed taking centre stage and froze as reality set in. She went into the bathroom, and I sat on the edge of the bed not knowing what to do. When she came out, she was wearing extremely sexy black lace underwear with very high heels, and she was holding a condom in her left hand. She started gyrating to some imaginary music pushing me backwards on the bed and rubbing herself against me, I tried to go with it, to relax, and enjoy this for what it was.

I've never worked out how to undress in a sexy way, she helped me, sitting on top and roughly taking charge. That's when I started to feel lost, emotional and quietly vulnerable in my pedestrian boxer shorts, I knew neither of us was up to this task. Images of

Maggie and Cassie flashed into my mind. When she started to kiss me, her hands were everywhere, it was too much too soon. I didn't want her skin on mine, I began to panic, she was too desperate, everything was moving too fast, I'm sure I could have been anyone to her.

I made a quick decision, grabbed my clothes, faked suddenly feeling ill from the fish and ran in my boxer shorts to the end of the corridor and into my room. Once inside I cried, releasing tension from the past few months, possibly years, then laughed at my naivety and inexperience with women who aren't my wife. I could imagine Maggie laughing at me kindly, understanding my clumsy attempt to move on, having no clue regarding women, then I thought of Cassie.

A headache hung above my ears for hours, pounding its fists on the side of my head, threatening to destroy a good night's sleep, not that I could switch off my thoughts. I nearly made a big mistake. I lay awake analysing how I got into the situation to prevent it from happening again, being flattered does not mean I should sleep with the first person to show an interest.

It couldn't have been more uncomfortable when I entered the breakfast room the next morning. She ignored me and began precisely cutting up her toast, her face was closed, and she was focused on the cutting. I ate alone, we couldn't look at each other.

I've named her the "Praying Mantis," they eat their mate after sex, I think she'd quite like to eat me as painfully as possible.

I could sense her rejection bouncing around the training room as her body bristled and tightly straightened itself every time someone said my name, all the softness was left on the bed sheets upstairs. Her neck flushed red when we had to speak, and she kept rolling her necklace between her thumb and index finger self-soothing her anger, furious with me, I don't think she's used to being turned down.

By the time we were leaving, the other three delegates were friends and planning to stay in touch and meet up. I was racing to escape the dagger landing in my back, running from the Praying Mantis afraid she might catch me and twist it in. Lesson learnt; I am not made for one-night stands.

On the drive home I debated telling someone about my foolishness, but who would I tell?

Mum, no, we don't have that sort of relationship although I know she'd try to help. The boys, no, it would be wrong.

Cassie?

There's a truckload of emotions to unpack with Cassie and I'm realising I need to stop taking her for granted. After the turmoil and incessant self-questioning have subsided, getting it wrong is helping me to discover what an idiot I've been so I can get it right. Last nights near miss has made it clear and cemented what's been standing in front of me, staring me in the face for months, but I didn't see it, perhaps I chose not to. I know my feelings for Cassie are real and I'm ready to talk about the future - if she'll have me.

2021 – Cassie

When Mike texts to say he's nearly done something very stupid, I think back to his drunken texts from his time in Spain with the boys.

"Having a great time, missing you" was the first one.

"Wish you were here" was the second.

I texted "Enjoy yourself" to both. I wanted to add, "Not too much though without me."

I've re-read them loads expecting the words to give me their true meanings. They could be what you'd send to a friend, but I want his words to mean more. I've never asked him about them, and he's never mentioned them, I don't know why I can't be honest and say something. Well, I do know why, I don't want to lose him. Having him as a good friend is better than not having him in my life, but I'm not sure I'm being fair to myself.

The week he returned from Spain we went out and he hugged me for ages, then he stepped back and looked directly at me and said,

"We should go on holiday and explore somewhere new," as if he wanted me to react. I didn't know what to say, I wasn't sure if he meant as friends or more than friends, I think I smiled and said maybe.

Before that conversation, I thought the feelings were one-sided, but when Mike said he wanted to move house and Dan asked if he was moving in alone, I didn't think Dan meant me until he looked my way. I was shocked and embarrassed as if we were keeping a secret from them. Mike will always be grieving for Maggie, I know that. I keep hoping eventually there might be a space for me.

We were getting closer, I thought. My feelings kept surfacing and sometimes I sensed he felt something but I convinced myself I was being ridiculous, making something out of nothing. I'm well-practised at hiding how I feel, scuttling home to sleep alone playing every comment over in my mind. It's like living on a seesaw with ultimate highs and bumpy lows, his trusted sounding board, my counselling skills make me perfect for this role in his life.

I'm like a well-behaved puppy who's grateful for any attention. Whenever Mike says he's calling in, I might as well be jumping on the sofa in the front window, barking, with my tail wagging, eager to accept a friendly pat or any crumb of affection and dog treat sent my way. I don't know if he's oblivious to how I feel, I'm beginning to despair at my behaviour, I don't want to be humiliated and ashamed.

So, when his text arrived after the Manchester course to say,

"I'm at the services on my way home from Manchester and I nearly did something very stupid" I respond calmly,

"What?"

"I went to the hotel room of a woman on my course." My heart sinks.

After deliberating for ages, I manage to reply with one word, "Why?"

"I don't know" arrives immediately.

"Did you want to be with her?"

"I thought I did"

I send "OK" and feel sick about what he might have done.

"It wasn't ok, I left when she got undressed"

"Didn't you like her?" I'm calmer now, how bad can it be if he left?

"No, it felt all wrong, I ran out of her room in my boxer shorts!"

I send a line of laughing emojis and he sends some blushing ones with two kisses at the end, I'm wondering if the extra kiss means anything, when he usually sends one if any.

I was trying to convince myself to be brave and speak to him about my feelings, but decided I'd wait until he'd settled after the move, give him time to adjust and cope with the big changes. I always do this, wait until after an event, put things off until later, give myself an excuse not to act, and now he tells me he was with another woman, briefly. I've made a joke of it, it's what I do and what he'd expect, now what?

No messages come through for over an hour, despite staring at my phone willing it to ping. I worry I've said the wrong thing and upset him.

"Can we talk?" pops up as I'm getting into bed for an early night.

"Yes"

"I think I have feelings for you"

"Think or know?"

"Know"

"I have feelings too"

My phone rings and his face fills the screen. We have the conversation I've imagined having for the last few years. I sit quietly and listen to Mike trying to articulate his feelings; he laughs with relief when he knows I feel the same and asks me out "officially" in a throwback move from the 1980s.

One day I'll let him know I've felt this way for years.

2021 – Sam

We are in our final year, heading rapidly towards the end of our student life and I have learnt a lot about myself and how to be a competent and caring nurse. The most important realisation, however, is that I want to be with Maisy forever.

I propose in the corner of the garden at the pub we visited on our first day at uni. I remember discussing what life would be like and trying to imagine this city as our home, acting confident before we felt it, and drinking too much to cover our nerves. We've been to this pub hundreds of times in the past few years and chosen to sit in this garden when the sun comes out.

Maisy says I need to finish my drink so we can go home before she will answer my question. It's not how it played out in my head, but she's smiling like it's Christmas or her birthday, so I'm pretty sure it's a yes.

At home, Maisy presents me with a book, it's full of our life. She's been collecting quotes, receipts, ticket stubs, and loads of things from our time together including photos of those we love. A book full of memories she's been saving for years, ready to make this proposal special for me too. I almost ruined it by asking,

"What would you have done with it if I hadn't proposed?" but in true Maisy style, she says that was never going to happen.

We re-live events, page by page, the last ten years bounce around like popcorn exploding in a pan, jumping and popping into life. Lots of brilliant times and some sad ones, this is the radiant Maisy I know so well, on and off the page, excited by life, smiling, optimistic and beautiful. A photo taken on my 16th birthday reminds me of the line I crossed when I stepped from child Sam into the unknown space of Alzheimer's, when the ground collapsed beneath me and my safe life became a minefield for a while. If it hadn't happened, I question what I would be doing with my life, I don't think I would have been doing this.

When we reach the final page, one word is written in huge pink flowery writing surrounded by hearts "YES!"

I've booked two nights away to celebrate our engagement, so all work anxiety and stress are cancelled. I thought we would phone everyone straight away to tell them, but Maisy surprises me by asking if we can keep the news to ourselves until tomorrow. I don't mention her mum and dad sort of know already because I phoned to ask if they'd be ok about me asking her while we were still at uni. Her dad said, if his "Sunshine Girl" was happy, he was happy. And my dad sort of knows because I asked his advice about getting down on one knee, which he insisted I must do, stressing,

"She'll find it romantic, it's not old-fashioned, and I don't care if you'll be in a public place, you must do it properly." He was right, she loved it.

We drive to the coast and check into a bed and breakfast close to the centre. Our accommodation stands out in a row of ice cream-coloured terraced houses, it's bright pink and has a small brightly painted blue boat in the front garden laden with shells, in case we're in any doubt this is the seaside. Maisy loves the house immediately.

The last time we were away was for my 18th, Dad paid for us to stay at a hotel in London, this is basic compared to that. Our room is at the front and faces the road, Maisy says it's cute, and she's the one who matters, I could sleep anywhere. The whole room is designed to remind you of the beach and the sea. You can see and hear the crashing sea through the trees, competing with the traffic to make the most noise, at night the sea wins.

I always underestimate how windy it is at the seaside. We start our adventure by going out to buy woolly hats from what Maisy calls the "Tat Shop," something to cover our ears and stop us from freezing to death, we'll never wear them in Newcastle.

We spend our days getting up late, eating a full English breakfast every morning, with me rejecting my mushrooms, pushing them onto Maisy's plate and swapping them for her grilled tomatoes. Then walking hand in hand on nearly empty beaches with fine powder-dry sand giving way underfoot, dipping our toes cautiously into the biting North Sea. We practice naming our children and agreeably disagree on the breed of dog we'll have; we visit castles and eat and drink like our food and drink supply might run out.

When we buy a kite I think of Dan, and the simple holidays we spent on the beach with Mum and Dad, persuading Dad to let us bury him up to his neck, and Mum getting up to help, the three of us manically digging for hours. Dad probably enjoyed the rest. As the wind twirls and twists snatching the kite upwards,

Maisy hangs on and I watch the red and yellow diamonds diving and flapping in the seal grey and pale blue sky, it's like my childhood is flying in the air. I'm tearful and brush the falling tears away blaming the wind, she holds me tightly.

Food features as a highlight in my memory bank, freshly fried doughnuts filled with jam, ice cream with raspberry and chocolate sauce, sprinkles and a flake if we were good. Eating fish and chips on the seafront with vinegar up my nose, nervously protecting them from the circling seagulls.

Every holiday we were allowed one trip to the amusement arcades with the pocket money my gran gave us to spend. I loved watching pennies roll in a line, betting and racing on the miniature plastic horses, I thought the more I shouted the more chance my horse would win. It's like exercising friendly ghosts, experiencing this with Maisy, as she wraps her arms around me, the memories wash over me like waves accompanied by the soothing soundtrack of the sea. I'll tell Dad how special those times were and what they meant to me when I see him.

Maisy says the freedom to do anything with no time constraints is exhilarating, escaping the pressure transforms us into the best version of ourselves. I hope Mum and Dad felt like this on our family holidays.

2021 - Shaun

I didn't know Ady was watching my Saturday night gig at the student union until he found me afterwards, propping up the bar. He hugged me like I was his long-lost friend, all sequins and glitter, with his latest spotty shag obediently following closely behind.

He shouted,

"I've sent a sample video of part of tonight's performance to an agent I know, if you want to get some work, you need to message him."

It's typical of Ady not to ask if that's ok with me, I'm secretly pleased and annoyed with his behaviour.

I contact the agent in the morning after checking him out online and he puts me on his books, it's that simple. Within a week I'm getting gigs in bigger clubs and performing regularly with a proper comedy slot not just seven minutes on the open mic circuit.

I didn't consult with anyone about my decisions, including Mum and Dad, there was no choice for them to make. I presented the situation as non-negotiable; it was not up for discussion. I would finish this degree and not carry on for a Master's, and I made it clear I didn't care about their opinion. In a predictable defensive Dad comment, he explained his position,

"I was checking how committed you were, purposefully using my arguments against a comedy career to test you to see if it was a passing phase or if you were serious."

I don't know if he's telling the truth, or if he feels bad about his lack of support, maybe it's his way of convincingly lying to himself, who cares?

I'm disciplined and juggling it all until I can concentrate full-time on comedy to see if I can make it work. The cash I get currently from gigging won't pay for what I want out of life, but it's not bad for a student. I'm energised by the comedy rush and knackered from studying for final exams, I'm in a massive sleep deficit, and my new gigs involve travelling further and later nights, but I've worked too hard to drop the degree or the comedy.

My material has developed, and I find it easy to craft jokes using an observational style with distorted truth thrown in there. I've realised accurate facts don't matter providing it's funny and I've dropped some of the detail. Apparently, the majority of comedians are introverts, appearing relaxed and quiet on the outside, screaming from the inside, finding their voice on stage and planning their escape from themselves, this is me.

Mum and Dad came to see me at one of the better bars I perform at, where your feet don't stick to the floor, and the beer is impressively served in glass not plastic. I wasn't as nervous as expected, I was in control, it was bizarre to see them together. I left out most of the "how parents damage you," section, I didn't think Mum could take it, but I left in tons of stuff about Dad.

I've replaced the Cocoa Pops card with an A4 sheet stuck to the stage, my usual set list looks like this.

My Life in Eight Stories
The early years – sad, gay, school life, parents
Dad – leaving for a younger model, inappropriate wife number two, wife number three
Living in my bedroom – reclusive gamer, adolescence, and TV years
Friends – quirky friends and friendship groups
Exams – my brilliance, expectations
Coming out – sleeping with a girl, girls and boys
Uni – new people and comedy career
Finish – car crash and relationships

Mum stood out in her flowery dress which she must have last worn in the '90s, amongst a sea of 20-year-olds, in cargo jeans, cropped tops and trainers. Dad fitted in, after all, he's paid to fit in anywhere.

We had a quick chat after the gig and Mum did her best to say the supportive stuff required of a parent, using words like different, interesting and brave. I think she left wondering where her son had gone.

2021 - Jody

I was looking forward to meeting James' sister for months before we turned into the drive at his parent's house. He hadn't said much about her, he wouldn't discuss her in detail but said she could be difficult.

As we got out of the car, on time, before her arrival, his dad joked,

"You know what Natasha's like, she's always late, she'll be preparing to make a grand entrance."

When Natasha walks in an hour later, she certainly makes her presence known, she is nothing like I expected her to be, she is awful.

I briefly glance at the black and white photographs of James and Natasha chronologically arranged in the hall, showing him almost as he is now, Natasha is unrecognisable. My mum would describe the woman standing in front of me as having a pinched face with a startled, irritated expression as if she'd smelt something unpleasant.

The face in the photos is relaxed and playful with the camera, and she appears to be enjoying herself. Her body has changed too, she now has pointy elbows and knees, I'm surprised her legs still support her, sticking out of her short black pencil skirt like dark brown matchsticks. I feel bitchy as these thoughts surface and

I push them down smiling at her widely, I'm impersonating the Cheshire Cat. I notice Murphy doesn't move towards her and she doesn't say hello to him.

I edge forward to hug her after she's thrown her bag across the floor, she steps away from me dramatically, maybe she's not a huggy type of person. Her rejection throws me off balance and I stand awkwardly while she looks down her nose dismissing my presence. I hear James whisper to her,

"Be nice," when he follows her into the dining room. I didn't know she wasn't nice.

When we sit down for lunch with his parents she doesn't look up, she half falls into the chair next to James and places her elbows on the table tapping her fingers on the placemat to an invisible tune, making sure she's the centre of attention. The mood is tense, and my brain returns to a well-rehearsed function and removes me from the situation. Random thoughts pass through my mind including, her hair needs conditioning, I wonder if we might become friends and I can recommend my brand, she's only five years older than me but we could easily be the same age looks-wise, we must have things in common and why is she out of place in this country home, her family home, what sort of person is she, she can't be that bad can she, she's related to James, and why does she seem cross I'm here, didn't she know I was coming?

Everything races out of control when I'm stressed. James can sense my nervousness and puts his hand on top of mine as my internal dialogue continues to distract me.

Natasha lives in Paris.

I imagined many versions of our first meeting and none of them played out this way. Their parents try to get her to speak, to "jolly her along," another of my mum's phrases she uses for tricky people, usually children under 10.

She finally acknowledges I exist and chooses to stare directly at me when she talks about James' ex-girlfriend and the local family she came from, stressing how "excellently" they all got on.

She is a bitch, with designer sunglasses perched on top of her split-ended slicked black hair and big Doc Martins worn with her entitled attitude, but I'm not scared.

Once she's tried and failed to upset me, she ignores me throughout the rest of lunch. Natasha is an odd mix of English and French and I'm not sure how much she says is true as she takes centre stage with her stories, enjoying the discomfort on her mum's face. I irritate myself by being overly smiley and friendly, nodding and trying to show an interest, killing her with kindness to make her like me, unfortunately, my upbringing won't let me be rude. It doesn't work, and when James and I are alone in bed that night he tries to reassure me and apologise for her behaviour.

"She has problems, it's not you, she's insecure underneath the act she puts on. Her life is complicated, and she likes to be the centre of everything to prove how well her life's going." I nod, it's good it's dark and he can't see my face.

At breakfast, I keep my distance and fuss Murphy, who's chosen to sit next to me, I love being picked by an animal. He's on the floor staring up at me with understanding eyes, I almost fall for his sympathetic face, but he's a labrador, it's not understanding, he's playing me for food. It's his "I'm starving nobody feeds me" look, I sneak him an organic sausage and instantly become his best friend. He's not been near Natasha since she arrived, I should have noticed earlier because animals sense things, she's too self-obsessed to pay him attention. Thankfully, she's only here for a few weeks and I'm going home tomorrow, I won't have to tolerate her much longer.

We drive to a pub for Sunday lunch, not the local one they normally go to, I nearly ask why but stop myself in time, the atmosphere is charged like lightning before a thunderstorm. Everyone seems on edge.

His parents glance anxiously at each other when Natasha orders an expensive bottle of wine and makes it clear she's not sharing. She picks through a side salad as we eat roast beef, and I observe how uncomfortable his usually relaxed parents are with their daughter. I'm dying to know what happened to her to make her behave this way, and question James when I get him alone in the pub car park.

He says he's not sure.

"She moved to Paris when I was 13. We were close when I was younger, she was like a second mum sometimes, when Mum was away building her career. I visited her in Paris for the first few years, we used to get on well, she was my big sister, and I loved being with her."

He puts their detachment now down to the age gap, I'm not convinced. I have plenty of time to study people working at the vets and relate people to animals regularly, amusing myself, by working out what animals they would be. Natasha would be a pecky, sulky, mean-spirited bird, a magpie. I realise a bird is not an animal, but you get the point. It's not always about looks, it can be the way a person speaks and moves that gives me the whole picture. You can learn a lot from watching people.

Small, cross, hopping man, late for his appointment, blaming the staff, gesturing wildly and complaining about parking – orangutan. A tiny lady with a shrill high voice, speaking quickly, drumming on the desk for attention, she's a mouse, racing up and down the floorboards in your loft annoying everyone. It passes the time.

We drive home from the pub, and I sit with James in his parent's show garden enjoying the late sun, Natasha joins us with another bottle of wine and a book.

James goes inside to find some nibbles and I sit quietly watching her work her way down the Malbec and wait for her to speak. I can see faint scars on her legs, perfect symmetrical lines, all horizontal, about 1cm apart, carefully healed, evidence of another life. Mini ladders, mid-thigh on show because her skirt has ridden up and she is less careful about tugging it down.

She sees me looking, meets my eyes, and silently dares me to ask about them, I don't. This lack of interest causes her to launch into me slurring about what a perfect life I've got without pausing for breath.

"You've done well getting James, snaring him, you must be talented at something to keep him interested, you're not as pretty as his last girlfriend, it's alright for you, quaint, provincial and sheltered from real life, the only child of doting parents, I bet you're the perfect daughter."

She doesn't know anything about me or my life, how dare she presume to know me?

She's making me mad, and I enjoy retaliating with the lowest points from my teenage pregnancy story to see the shock on her face. I use my painful experience to get the reaction I want and immediately regret telling her. It feels cheap and wrong to score points like this. I worry she'll tell her parents, and they'll change their opinion of me, I get up to leave. She grabs my arm, says she's sorry and asks me to sit back down, I hesitate, then sit. I am suspicious and guarded with my answers when she asks about me, and I disclose the bare minimum, I'm not sure she's listening anyway.

When I've finished speaking, she launches into her story, it's like she's reading from a book. Her voice is rehearsed, it's flat and detached without emotion, as if she's delivered this to several therapists and she's bored repeating it. Her eyes narrow and show some pain, she keeps swallowing when she mentions letting her parents down.

"I loved languages and got straight A's and A*'s in every subject when I took my GCSEs. But for sixth form, I had to move schools because my school didn't have one, that's when things started to go wrong. At the new school, I was no longer at the top of everything, and I was used to overachieving, that's who I was. I had no friends, and the pressure got to me. I pushed myself to become head girl, voted for by the teachers, I thought that would make me popular, but it had the opposite effect.

Before my A levels I had a meltdown and cutting my legs was a way to relieve the pressure, to be in control, except I was never in control. I didn't get the grades I needed for the two top language universities and everywhere else felt like second best, so I dropped out completely. My dad's never forgiven me."

At this point, she starts to cry, I reach over to hold her hand, it's cold. I rub it between my palms like my mum would do to me, and I think of injured birds.

We sit quietly until she continues to tell me how she ended up living in Paris, rambling and repeating parts as she continues to drink.

"My dad knew someone via his business connections who agreed to take me on as an office junior at his Paris branch, my French was excellent, so I went there to start again and worked hard to become his P.A. Work is all I've had in my life for a long time. I'm jealous of you and James, why can't it be me with a successful relationship? I know you're the one, I know my brother, and I need time to adjust, we used to be close, I don't know what happened."

I've read enough celebrity stories online and their biographies and self-help books, so when she says,

"It's as if they sent me away for failing," I'm not surprised.

Although she admits part of her wanted to go, to run away, what she needed was for them to ask her to stay.

She keeps repeating -

"They should have known I didn't want to go to another country alone. It was like I was being punished. I was still a little girl inside."

She speaks in a childish, whiney voice when she says this and her arms wrap themselves protectively around her body hugging her knees and creating a tight ball, subconsciously shrinking herself. She is very drunk. She's not a mean girl, she's a sad and lonely one.

I leave her outside rocking with her eyes closed and go in to get a blanket, wondering where James is. I find him fast asleep in a dining room chair and wake him up. He lets his mum know she's outside and she takes her the blanket and we go to bed.

The evening's conversation with Natasha plays between us uneasily, we are cautiously batting it backwards and forwards as I learn about his family, we whisper and try not to disagree. I've got no chance of falling asleep. I can't accept her view of their parents, but she seemed genuinely upset, do his parents know how she feels? James says not to believe everything she says. I can't stop thinking I could help her.

The next morning, she doesn't appear for breakfast, and we leave without saying goodbye. His parents are embarrassed and make excuses for their daughter, I make sure they know it doesn't matter to me and thank them for a super time.

I wonder if my parents have made excuses for me.

2021 - Sam

We are hosting a dinner party at our house, technically it's James' house but you know what I mean. Apparently, it's what people do to celebrate their engagement, and it feels very grown up. James and Jody have agreed to help, we've invited Dad, Cassie, and Maisy's mum and dad. Dan is bringing a mystery date and

Shaun is coming too, alone, which is probably a good idea after Ady.

Maisy is excited and we seem to be making enough food for the whole street. She's chosen an Italian menu, and it turns out that Lasagne is a lot more complicated than we thought it would be to construct. Five hours of cooking later, James, Jody and I are wishing we'd arranged to go out. She's determined to make it an event of restaurant standards, it's like she wants to prove to our parents she's old enough to be engaged, as if this is a test of her future wife status. The rest of us are trying to reassure her it will be fine, which isn't landing well.

"I want it to be perfect, it shouldn't be this difficult." She raises her voice sharply as she bangs the oven door shut.

"Nobody will care. They're coming to celebrate and spend time with us, and you're not a professional chef so they won't be expecting great food." I thought this was a reassuring response.

"Thanks for the vote of confidence." The white sauce isn't the only thing about to boil over.

Everything's matching in varying shades of pink. Tall pink candles run down the centre of the table in three alarmingly loud pink candelabras. Pink serviettes are neatly folded on pale pink plates, and little pink dishes I didn't know we had have appeared filled with olives, crisps and mixed salted nuts, artfully arranged, waiting expectantly like the rest of us, to be allowed to eat them. We've got name cards placing Jody and Shaun at opposite ends of the table, they speak but it's awkward.

Maisy is losing her sense of humour and snaps at Jody when she tries to eat a crisp. James and I escape the kitchen and are opening a beer when the doorbell rings half an hour before anyone is due to arrive. It's her mum and dad with a huge bunch of Sunflowers, and Maisy's not changed out of her cooking clothes yet. When her dad hugs her and tells her to calm down, I'm not sure if she's going to yell at him for being early or cry.

He forces her out of the kitchen, and they take over and I'm happy to let them, the grown-ups are in charge again. I follow her into the bedroom and make a silly face, mimicking her pose with my hands on my hips and an exaggerated frown. She doesn't understand where the monster appeared from and laughs at herself and me, then sighs,

"Don't ever let me do this again, it was a terrible idea," and smiley Maisy returns as she gets dressed for the evening.

Dad, Cassie and Shaun arrive on time and Dan arrives 20 minutes late with chocolates and the girl he met in Spain. Dan pulls me to one side and apologises,

"We've driven around the block three times because Eva's apprehensive about meeting everyone, she desperately wants to make a good impression."

I can see she's important to him, he's looking at her and me anxiously. You wouldn't know she was worried, she's full of smiles and deep in conversation with Cassie now. She looks a bit like a young version of Mum from the photos I've seen, with the same petite build and long dark hair, but when she speaks a soft Scottish voice comes out and the illusion is broken.

Her mum is from Scotland and her dad is from Oxford, Scotland definitely won the battle of the accents. They kept seeing each other after Spain, and Dan being Dan didn't say much to me or Dad about it being serious. Maisy raises her eyebrows, and I raise mine back at her as Eva puts her arm through Dans possessively.

The evening is filled with reminiscing, re-living our childhood stories and explaining our connections. I look at each person seated at the table partway through beer number four, taking in the love and support surrounding me, and think of Mum in the nursing home, at Greenacres. Whenever I start to feel content, relaxed or very happy I think of Mum. Everything is perfect until that loose thread, the disconnected part of me, reminds me my family are not all here. I'm used to it now, at first it stopped me from enjoying anything, and guilt played a big part. I can quietly acknowledge the intrusion now and use it to make me a better son, to push me to visit her and ease my conscience. It is possible to be happy and sad at the same time, I asked Dad, and he said he felt the same way when I left home.

I go to join Shaun who is usually an observer at these things, and he taps my shoulder and says,

"I wish I had a family like yours."

I know what he's trying to say so I don't mention the weight of the gaping hole I can feel.

We toast the future, and Dad passes Maisy a small purple box.

"Sam's mum would want you to have this."

Inside the box is a silver spinning ring I recognise; it was one of Mum's favourites. She used to wear it on her thumb and spin the silver band around the middle when she was thinking, I picture her easily now, as if the memory was from last week not years ago. I know Mum gave Dad some of her jewellery when she was diagnosed with Alzheimer's and asked him to share it with the family when the time felt right. It's a sobering moment, and the room falls silent as Maisy tries the ring on.

I'm surprised to hear my voice toasting Mum, my body is standing up on its own, I'm not sure what I'm doing. They follow my lead and stand, it's a joyful clinking of glasses saluting Mum, until I glance at Dan. We can't meet each other's eyes; I don't want to fall to pieces.

Maisy presents dessert with an accomplished look on her face, and she receives a round of applause, we're banging our cutlery on the table and stamping our feet in united approval.

We agree the Tiramisu is the finest we've ever tasted, and Maisy looks like she's won first prize on TV's Bake Off, bowing to her audience and loving every minute. Dessert wine follows because we need more sugar, and Maisy, still in hostess mode, diligently checks we're using the right glasses.

The evening ends with our parents and Cassie getting a taxi back to their hotel. The rest of us stay up most of the night dancing, chatting and playing drinking games. Eva's accent becomes strongly Scottish which we find hysterical, and we all reveal more about ourselves with every drink.

Eva and my brother are evidently very much a couple, I have never seen him like this, he's openly kissing her, touching her leg and stroking her face, it's great he thinks she's hot, but it's awkward to watch. He mentions they're planning to move in together not far from Dad when Dan starts his new job, teaching at a junior school, my brother never fails to surprise me.

When Shaun tells his car crash story it's the most memorable story of the night, he's learnt to laugh at himself, and I'm pleased for him, the old Shaun would never have done this. He's relishing the laughs from his audience and putting himself firmly in the spotlight, he's lapping it up and confidently batting back our heckling like a pro. My introverted old best friend is a comedian.

I fall into bed at 6am and look at the ceiling, I can't sleep. The house is silent but my brain won't stop, it's like a hamster on a wheel doing a workout on repeat. I think about whether Cassie will be moving in with Dad soon, how he's moved on, changing his job, and leaving our house. I try to squash that happy and sad feeling again. Maisy is snoring, she'll be terrible when she wakes up, she can't drink much, and she's mixed her drinks.

I get up and start to tidy around the sleeping bodies sprawled in the lounge. I'm enjoying the calm after the chaos, and the process of getting things in order. I realise I'm turning into my dad.

2021 – Maisy

I'm expecting an injured kitten to limp through the door when I open it, after Jody's description of Natasha. She is nothing like Jody's description.

I'd laid out my hair and make-up products in case she wanted to get ready here. Jody said she's lonely and needed friends. I was curious to know what James' sister would be like, so getting ready together for a night out seemed like a fun idea. I thought we'd be casually chatting about nothing important with a bottle of fizzy rosé, working out where we wanted to go and discussing who might be in our local bars, basically just enjoying being girls. However, she looks like she's primed for a catwalk and presents herself with the confidence of someone who knows they look impressive, in no way does she need rescuing.

She's wearing the tightest, shortest, shiny black one-piece playsuit with a big metal zip up the front, the highest black stilettos with red bows, and a pair of massive Ray-Bans covering half her face. She has flashy red lipstick on, and several gold chains, the longest one has a chunky "N" on it, and it lands between her fake (I'm guessing) boobs.

She reminds me of some girls in an '80s video my mum used to watch; she looks amazing but won't fit into our usual student bars. Jody says she looks like another person compared to the tear-stained Natasha she left weeks earlier in James' parent's garden. I believe everyone should be themselves and do what they want, as long as they don't hurt others, be what they want but try to be kind, and wear what they want, it's their body, they get to choose, but I wish she was wearing something else. She instantly makes me uneasy, like I'm a little girl playing at life and she's all grown up and has everything figured out, despite what Jody said, Natasha is intimidating, she has her claws out and I can feel that she's poised and in position to pounce.

She holds my shoulders firmly and air kisses me on each cheek, forcing me from one side to another so I sway slightly off balance, and she says, "Bonjour darling," as if she's French, which she's not, she pronounces darling with a drawn out double "hh" in the middle for effect, "darhhling" as she sails past me into our lounge.

She sees James, he gets the same treatment, and I overhear her say,

"So, this is what you get as Mummy and Daddy's favourite, a whole house!"

He doesn't answer, his look across at me says, "I told you to stay out of it, I didn't want her here, but you and Jody pushed it."

I brightly smile and mouth "Wow."

She turns to face me directly,

"And you share your house with your friends, how fabulous for them, I hope they're paying you something, you've always been a soft touch." Then she laughs as if she's told a hilarious joke. I'm trying not to dislike her but she's making it impossible.

Sam walks out of our bedroom and does a double-take as she kisses him, pulling him tightly forward before he knows what's happening. I've never been jealous, but unfamiliar prickles race up my arms and down my back. They make me walk across the lounge to stand next to him and I take his hand, lacing my fingers through his.

Sam, James and Natasha move into the kitchen, when Jody and I go to get ready. She's answering Sam's questions about Paris as I assess my pathetic make-up selection, lined up neatly waiting. I'm embarrassed I thought she might want to use it.

I try on a dozen outfits and throw each one angrily on the bed. I look ordinary and boring compared to her, predictable Maisy, it's like comparing a strutting peacock to I don't know what, something less showy, she's the expensive boutique and I'm the charity shop. Jody doesn't know what to say, and I don't know why I'm behaving this way, she watches as clothes pile on top of each other covering the bed.

We leave my bedroom an hour later and no one comments on how we look, no attention-grabbing entrance for us. Jody looks cute in a fitted green dress, and I decided on a short pink denim one with long boots and black tights, I'm more dressed up than I normally would be, but I'm not happy. Sam smiles and says, "At last," making me madder.

The first bar "Solo" is ok, Natasha comments in a condescending way,

"It's quaint, very different to Paris."

It's noisy and we can't talk which suits me fine. We're on our way to the club when we walk past a wine bar we've never been in, it's not the sort of place we'd go and it's too expensive for us students. She says it looks nice and pulls Sam with her towards the window. James tactfully tries to explain it's expensive and she replies,

"It's not a problem, I'll pay for some wine, it's the least I can do after you've invited me out, I'm here for a fabuleux time," which means fabulous in French in case you didn't know.

We follow her like sheep and squash into a plush velvet-lined booth, she manages to sit next to Sam. I'm opposite him at the end of the table by the wall next to Jody. Natasha is confident and keeps putting her hand on his arm, patting and stroking him and laughing at everything he says, she's attentive and predatory. She knows exactly what she's doing. I don't know if he's flattered, naive or being ultra-polite. I want to pick up a steak knife and stab her. She ignores me except for one superior smile when I glare back. Jody rapidly chats to fill the gap in conversation trying to cover the awkwardness.

It doesn't get any better at the club, she's an accomplished dancer, obviously, and people move to make an outer circle around her and watch as she grinds and twerks, she provides a compelling floor show. Natasha is a performer, mainly to men, she's manipulative and I dislike her intensely.

When we get home, I want to go straight to bed. Sam says he's going to stay up for a while with James and Nat (he calls her Nat now; their relationship has moved on!) to listen to music. Nat has a variety of interesting French indie artists on her phone allegedly, I don't say anything. I lay awake listening to every sound, making sure I hear three voices, trying to stay awake until Sam comes to bed. I'm super mad at myself for inviting her into our lives.

I must have fallen asleep because the shouting wakes me up. Two voices, Natasha and James arguing like children do, not caring who hears, the gloves are off. Then I hear Sam trying to calm them down and Jody's voice, she must have got up. Natasha is wrapped in a blanket and crying dramatically on the sofa when

I walk in. James looks uncomfortable pacing up and down, fingers digging holes in his pockets. I watch her concentrate and pick the skin around the gel nail on her middle finger, bite it, then suck the blood when it bleeds.

Sam comes over and takes my hand, leading me back to bed. He says we'll talk about it in the morning, then infuriates me by falling asleep while I lay awake thinking, we'll talk about what?

In the morning Jody and I are up first, closely followed by Sam and James. It's like everyone knows a secret that I don't, I missed the e-mail. I've never felt left out with my friends so when no one mentions last night, I ask what the shouting was about. Sam puts the kettle on, he's moving slowly, noisily releasing air, blowing out and dropping his shoulders as he walks.

"It's not a big thing, we were all drinking loads, and it was a stupid mistake."

I watch Jody bite her bottom lip as Sam delivers the line, she doesn't need to speak, she knows how I'll react to whatever they're going to tell me.

We sit on the sofa, mugs of tea clasped in our hands, and everyone looks at me nervously, except Natasha, who is still in bed I presume? Sam and James retell the evenings events, making it clear nothing happened, I don't think they'd stand up to police interrogation, tripping over each other's words, but I know Sam is telling the truth.

Natasha had had too much to drink, bless her, and decided Sam might enjoy a lap dance, ending with her sitting on his knee trying to kiss him, and then the shouting started. She'd stripped down to her underwear and an image of her naked skinny legs wrapping him up like a bow on a Christmas present fleetingly passes through my mind.

James gets up from the sofa to make more tea and Jody and Sam say he was incensed with her behaviour, asking her to have some self-respect and shouting,

"You always ruin everything because you're jealous of everyone. I know you'd love me to mess up to make you feel accepted but it's not going to happen. Mum and Dad have done what they can to help you, the prodigal daughter, and I'd like to know what gives you the right to interfere in my life and upset my friends. You have no personality of your own, the more you drink the more you become other people, you don't know who you are anymore, and I don't recognise you as the big sister I grew up with, where did she go?"

Jody says this isn't the first time he's spoken these words; he kept stressing how she needs to get over the mess she's made of her life and take some personal responsibility.

James returns, puts the drinks down, and continues to tell us she's selfish, self-absorbed and enjoys causing trouble and that's why she has no friends.

"She needs to be the most popular person in the room, the centre of attention, the cleverest, the thinnest, the most attractive, the greatest dancer, with her everything's a competition."

James is mortified and embarrassed by his sister's behaviour but not surprised. He ends the character assassination with his head in his hands and Jody trying to reassure him it will be ok.

I walk calmly to the kitchen to put in some toast, playing for time before I allow myself to speak. I'm practising my relaxed breathing like we do at the hospital before we deliver bad news. Jody follows me in, I want to yell at her that it's her fault for bringing Natasha into our lives. Except it was me who insisted we went out after Jody explained what happened when she met Natasha and described how sad and lonely she was. James struggled with the idea, the good guy that he is wants everyone to get along, but his protective nature was conflicted, and he kept telling us it was a bad idea, but we weren't listening. Ultimately, he didn't want anyone to get hurt. It was the first time I'd witnessed them properly argue and I was surprised to hear him shout. I shouldn't have got involved, I'm always trying to solve everyone's problems, and I need to stop interfering.

I don't trust myself to say anything and butter my toast with bubbling anger, scraping it furiously. I pick up my plate to take it back to bed and three pairs of eyes follow me from a safe distance.

Sam cautiously comes into the bedroom and gets into bed with me, I'm tempted to turn away. He's composed and reasonable and trying to be reassuring, dismissing last night as no big deal and joking about how irresistible he is. I ask him if he thinks she's attractive, he pauses,

"Yes, in an older woman kind of way." I nod and continue,

"Do you like her?"

He knows what I mean and looks at me like I've lost my mind. He reaches across the barrier I've mentally created and pulls me towards him, I relax in the space between his neck and his shoulder. We're back on track, of course he doesn't "like her, like her," he's in love with me. A familiar swirl of bubbly happiness rises inside me like an orange lava lamp switching on.

We spend most of the day in bed sleeping. When the front door closes late afternoon and I know she's definitely left, I do a happy dance on the bed and treat Sam to some of my naked moves. I should thank her; we had outstanding sex that night.

2021 – Mike

I set off for the nursing home on autopilot, distracted by questions without a definite answer. I've had a restless night working out what I want to say to Maggie and why I'm saying it in the first place when she won't understand. I've practised the order in which I want to tell her things, like I rehearse what I'm going to say before I phone the doctor.

Maggie has been living with Alzheimer's for years, through each stage from diagnosis to where she is now, I've tried rightly or wrongly to hide some of my grief, anger and fear from her and the overwhelming sense of helplessness. I carry my guilt, she knew I would do this, for not being able to care for her at home, but it's not crushing me anymore. Moving to the nursing home was her choice, the right choice, the boys and I have managed to move on, which is what she wanted. I re-live our decisions when I can't sleep and wonder how many years she has left, convincing myself we could have coped.

I can't find a concrete right or wrong answer about what to say in my analytical brain, no black or white just lots of grey. It's not helpful. I keep questioning why I want to speak to Maggie, am I subconsciously asking for her forgiveness or permission, or am I expecting her to agreeably accept my choice to move forward without her, which is ridiculous as we all had to move forward years ago.

Cassie's voice joins the internal dialogue,

"If you need to tell her then do it, be honest. Even though Maggie can't understand, you were honest in your marriage and trusted and respected each other, perhaps it's something you need to do for you."

Technically I'm breaking my marriage vows, maybe I'm looking for absolution?

I pull into Greenacres as I have done hundreds of times, it's not raining this morning, so I park at the far side of the car park to get my steps in. Mum would call my mood melancholy. On Google, I look up the dictionary definition of melancholy to delay me further. "Feeling or expressing sadness," my mum would be right.

Walking into Maggie's room I'm apprehensive, this is nothing new, I never know what sort of day she's having, she's unpredictable and sometimes I'm frightened of her, before she moved here she occasionally lashed out as the illness took her further away from us.

I half turn the chair next to her and sit down, she's looking out across the garden, and I'm looking at the side of her face. She doesn't acknowledge my presence. I'm used to the frustration that comes with a one-way conversation. Wordlessly she points at a robin, I glance and smile, not a smile really, more of a memory that's dropped in to throw me off course. Maggie always said…

"Robins represent passed loved ones being close by, their spirit is sent to comfort you." How I wish I could hear her say that again. I don't think I ever believed it, but Maggie wanted to. We were so happy.

I start my updates like I'm confessing to a priest, with no response, working up to the hardest part, putting off the thing I've come to say, rambling to avoid it. I don't want Maggie to think badly of me, to think

I'm being unfaithful. I'm talking to myself, whatever I say to her isn't going in, but it seems irrationally important to say it.

How do you tell your wife whom you will always love deeply that you are starting a new life and committing to another woman?

"You would have loved Sam and Maisy's engagement party, everyone being together, they are such a loving couple. She's exactly what you would have wanted for him. She's quirky and a lot of fun, obsessed with pink, and she cooked some great food. She brings Sam out of his shell when he needs it and helps him relax. He's learning to take life less seriously, she's so supportive, he's determined like you though and passionate about making a difference, he sees injustice everywhere.

I felt it was the perfect occasion to give Maisy your spinning ring, I hope I got that right. Listening to them plan their future reminded me of us with our hopes, dreams, and bucket lists, and how exciting it was to make plans with you. I'm thankful we were blindly naive to our fate, I miss you. I miss the easy way we communicated, knowing what you were thinking, and the times you knew how I felt before I could put it into words. I'm not sure anyone will ever know me as well as you did. I want to be us again.

We have two exceptional children thanks to you, well technically speaking, us, I can hear you telling me off for being pedantic.

Dan's surprised me by how quickly he's settled down with Eva, you'd like her, and I think they are right together, two peas in a pod finishing each other's sentences. If we hadn't gone to Spain, it might never have happened. I'm pleased they're going to be living near me, you'd be so proud, he's a teacher like you were. Although the children give him the runaround, he loves it, you would have got them into shape.

Jody is finally with someone suitable after a few false starts, I know how much you liked her. She's turned into a lovely young lady, more confident and animal mad, James is clearly besotted with her. She'd drive me mad, constantly chatting.

The biggest surprise is Shaun trying to become a comedian, out of all their friends we would have never believed that quiet, serious, almost rude Shaun would choose comedy as a career, I know you weren't keen on him. I think he's had a lot to cope with, I don't think his mum and dad are very pleased with him according to Sam. We could never have predicted how everybody's story would change, lives full of ordinary and extraordinary events, especially ours.

Do you remember Cassie?

She helped you when you came to enquire about moving to Greenacres, you liked and trusted her, I like her too and we've become… well… more than friends, and she's moving in with me at my new apartment, I hope that's ok."

One long sentence delivered then I weep for us, unable to control the enormity of my suppressed pain, knowing I will never get over losing the love of my life.

Although I'm moving on, I am still grieving for Maggie and me and the life we lost. I worry for her future which will be short, and for how painfully this cruel disease will end her life.

She turns her hands noisily slapping one on top of the other, and I notice a small heart drawn in black biro on her left palm. I wonder if she drew it and if not, who could have done it?

I don't feel any better. Maybe I expected to be absolved of all my guilt if I told her. It was crucially important to square it with myself and the right thing to do for her. Is there ever a right thing?

For self-preservation, I hang onto the lie -

"At least she knows." She doesn't of course.

I get up to leave, Maggie gets up, steps forward and puts out her hand. We shake hands as if we've just concluded a business meeting, and then she smiles. It's the smile I remember from the day we met, broad, open and welcoming, she had me at "hello" all those years ago. The mischief rarely dances in her eyes anymore but it's there and she nods, it probably doesn't mean anything, but it might. Instinct takes over and I raise my arms and move towards her for a hug. Her eyes narrow, she's alarmed, her hands cover her head as she takes a step away from me.

I walk towards the door focusing on my footsteps, hesitate, then turn briefly to look back at the stranger.

2021 – Cassie

As he gently takes my face in his hands, I know this is it. I've got no make-up on and I'm hot and sweaty from helping him decorate. I'm tempted to make a joke about picking his moment, but I don't want to spoil it.

We've been painting the bedrooms at his new apartment for most of the week, not much call for a made-up face, and we've talked and talked about our lives and the letters. I've not spent this amount of time with anyone for years.

We go over how Maggie's mum coped with her situation and survived, sheltering Maggie while keeping and living with secrets all her life. The boys and their partners feature in our conversation and Mike talks about the hopes he has for them. We are content painting during the day, stopping for regular cups of tea and coffee and eating meals together, simple ordinary tasks that mean everything to me.

Mike's finding a way to accept the past and change the family story he knew so well. I think he feels like he's leaving Maggie even further behind, I reassure him that we'll remember her together. In his mind, he needs to write another ending from the one he was expecting with Maggie, but he is ready for our adventure I'm sure of that.

This is the start of us, Cassie and Mike, he says he's looking forward to the future, our future, after the last few years I thought this might never happen. I was right to wait for him though, whatever this is I know we're both serious about making it work, and this is where I'm meant to be, he is my world.

He's teaching me that being vulnerable doesn't equal weakness, in fact, it's quite the opposite. After spending years on my own I think my family would describe me as a bit sharp and spikey, and definitely cynical and sarcastic about relationships. They don't know this softer Cassie, Mike is the one getting to see her, he is changing me for the better.

He kisses me deeply, conveying his feelings with passion, and a part of me I didn't know I was missing feels complete. I'm not the biggest fan of cheesy films and books so starring in my own soppy movie is a bit awkward for me. We've taken things slowly, holding hands and brief kisses, this is different, deep, another level, I've never felt this way.

When he asks me to move in, he says,

"I love you," for the first time.

"I love you too," I reply, as he folds me into him. We don't need to say anymore.

2021 - Mike

As I kiss Cassie, she knows I mean what I say, the time is right, I want to make a life with her. Her face relaxes and the smile I have come to know so well spreads across her quizzical face. I trace her freckles with my fingertip, her makeup usually covers most of them. It's like these freckles are special, they've been hiding, waiting for me to get close enough to see them.

She's always seen me, and every side of me has shown up since we met again at Greenacres, like rolling the dice, I've been unpredictable and she's still here, waiting. I love her. I see her now for the person she is, and I want her to be mine.

Cassie arrives in her packed car with the things she needs to move in with me. I laugh out loud when I spot a pink hula hoop perched on top of the pile and silently acknowledge we have many things to discover, like peeling an onion, we are only a few layers in.

I help her unload what she considers her essential items and when we are nearly finished, she presents me with a framed picture of the poem "Time" she found in one of Maggie's cookery books when we were clearing out for the move. Maggie's copy had been ripped from a Woman's Own magazine and the page had the date at the top. It was from the week she was diagnosed. Cassie said it was sandwiched between a recipe for a quiche Lorraine and a treacle sponge, neither of which I can remember Maggie cooking.

It has been beautifully transposed and expertly written, with soft illustrations featuring a beachscape in muted colours and dogs, hearts and wine glasses dotted around the edge. At the bottom, Maggie had handwritten "WEAR PURPLE NOW!" and Cassie's made sure this line is there in handwriting as close to Maggie's as possible.

She's had it framed to match the other poem "*Warning*"* which I'd already put up in the kitchen, Maggie and I had this up throughout our married life. It talks about wearing purple and being outrageous in old age, this one is its younger sister, it's sad and less hopeful, but it meant something to Maggie.

Cassie and I stand and look at the poems hanging side by side on the newly painted wall and everything feels right. Any apprehension I had regarding Cassie moving in was fleeting and had more to do with her coping with me, than me thinking I could be making a mistake.

It helps that we can talk about Maggie, and the boys can talk freely about their mum. She's helped us to do this and stopped it from being awkward, and she understands me. We will ride the storms together, but she will never be a replacement for Maggie.

They are exceptional and unique women, comparing them would be ridiculous, like comparing the first car you loved with all your heart and thought you'd keep forever, to a completely different model you love because your children fit into it, and you think it's safer for them. Loving them both for different reasons but love, nonetheless.

I don't underestimate how lucky I am to have found this kind of love twice.

* *Warning* – Jenny Joseph.

Time

I stand in the sea in my flip-flops when there's ice on top of the dunes

And imagine the children they play with are mine and pretend to take them home soon.

I smile at every passer-by and gently pat their dogs

And slip and slide on the green seaweed like silky hair on a brush.

I live on porridge and pizza and eat chocolate for my tea

Order gravy and chips with fine red wine

Then sing loudly and dance on the grass with the moon

And stand in the rain till my knickers are wet

And drip on the doormat back home.

I watch people around me carefully, for signs they are coming undone

And squeeze those I love too long and too hard to imprint them with my heart.

I hear snippets of conversations, from lives that I'll never live

The big hand ticks and I want it to stop to freeze me in time for a bit.

I've learnt that life is precious
But I did know this before
And not everyone's happy when you succeed
Well two fingers up to them!

When I pass a hearse, it reminds me, that my story is shorter than most
I've rented this body and they want it back, my ticket is long overdue.

WEAR PURPLE NOW!!

Acknowledgements

Thank you to Craig my supportive and patient husband, particularly for his insightful feedback and editing skills he didn't know he possessed. His ability to argue for or against a comma is legendary.

James Wake for critiquing with honest and constructive feedback even though he had a bad cold.

Daniel Wake, Alisia Angel, Holly Feeney and Sophie Wake, your early insights helped immensely to understand the voice of my characters.

Matthew Bird for his typesetting skills and vast knowledge of almost everything book related. And to Michael Heppell and all at *Write That Book*.

Finally, thank you to my friend Laurie Gray for selling us her seaside home and for lending me her fabulous name.

Sally Measom's debut "Fiction" book

Sally Measom's debut "Self-Help" book

Available from Amazon

About the Author

Sally Measom

Northumberland is my home. I am constantly excited and uplifted by the beautiful beaches surrounding me. The spirit of the people and the place is infectious and perfect for the creative process.

I have three amazing children and a husband who is still seasick!

Thank You for reading *Eleven Letters*,
I hope you enjoyed it.

Pick up a copy of *Five Words* from
www.livelifeyourway.co.uk or Amazon
and discover where this story started.

Praise for Sally Measom

"A book that is as devastating as it is hopeful. Sally gets into the heads and hearts of a family dealing with an impossible challenge. A moving read."

Suzy Walker
Journalist for The Telegraph and The Guardian

Other books by Sally Measom

Five Words

Live Life Your Way